Vile Blood

Published by Jen Golembiewski

http://jengolembiewski.weebly.com/

Follow me on Twitter: @JenGolembiewski

Like my Facebook Page:
http://www.facebook.com/vilebloodseries

Rate/Review this book at:
http://www.goodreads.com/book/show/25161610-vile-
blood

Dedication

For Gabriel, wish I could have met you.

"Not every fire starts with an explosion, most simply begin with a match."

-Jen Golembiewski

Prologue

The night sky lit up like fire as masses of unholy magic blazed over the screams of the people. They had been awakened from their peaceful slumber by creatures from the darkest depths of shadows. Their barriers were broken; the beasts had crossed; now all they could do was fight back. The bodies of person after person fell busted to the ground, with every scream and tragedy witnessed by the violet eyes of a teenage girl, hidden in a wooden crate by her grandfather as a last attempt to save his only kin.

No amount of training could have prepared her for a battle like this; outnumbered and overpowered, every member of her clan unable to stand long. Fallen comrades within view no longer looked recognizable; all familiar definition had gone from their faces. Soon her clan disappeared from the fight altogether and only these demons remained. Some walked like men with the fangs and claws of monsters. Others were more deceiving and could only be distinguished by the glowing tinge in their eyes.

The girl watched as the creatures confirmed the death of every person, some taking trophies with them, others just pleased with the kill. She held her breath as one grew near to check the body of her former playmate. As it leaned down she could see the scales on its face, not quite like a reptile but more like that of a pine cone; it looked as though it was made up of the forest itself. It suddenly cocked its head and sniffed the air. It moved away from the body and stepped closer to the crate. It continued to sniff, and the girl realized that the creature had picked up her scent. She couldn't run without bringing further attention to herself, all she could do was wait it out and hope the beast gave up its search. It stepped closer to her, and she saw its glowing red eyes settle on her crate. She knew then that it was aware of her presence; there would be no more hiding.

Chapter 1

Sarain rose from her bed; another bad dream had disturbed her sleep. Most nights were un-restful, memories of gruesome sights she had seen over the years haunted her as if still real. She paced throughout her small dwelling; not quite a home, her job wouldn't let her settle to make one. The rooms were dark from the lack of windows. It was still day, but Sarain found it easier to fortify her quarters if there were minimal possible entries. There were no personal effects or decorations hung about - just the necessities, and few at that. No mirrors or reflective surfaces; this was a must for her, because to the average person they may be harmless, but to Sarain they showed much more than a mere replica of its surroundings. They showed the same horrific images that she tried to escape from in her dreams, only clearer.

Sarain made herself a simple meal, nothing fancy but adequate. Soon she would have to work. This was all a part of her daily tradition; many procedures, though some came unexpected, all left Sarain's life feeling motionless. She had become robotic over the years. No friends, no family, and few acquaintances, but she didn't long for more, all she wanted was to destroy them all - every last monster that waited in the darkness.

Sarain was born a hunter, trained since childhood; she was raised learning of demons and their weaknesses, sunlight being the obvious. These creatures were damned into darkness; while not all demons can be killed by sunlight, they all do have an aversion to it. Another weakness is to holy emblems; the ankh works best of all. Resembling a cross, it is an ancient Egyptian symbol for life. It holds the most power compared with all the other emblems since it is the most recognized and feared symbol amongst demons. Holy emblems wouldn't kill a demon, but would repel them on sight, and to the weaker of their kind it would burn. Sarain kept an old tarnished ankh, passed down from her ancestors, always around her neck.

She quickly dressed, all in black; this made it easier to hide in the shadows and keep from being seen. She grabbed her freshly sharpened machete and strapped it to her side, then donned a trench coat to hide it. It was warm out, but Sarain knew that she would attract a lot more attention being seen with a machete than she would being overdressed. She needed to blend in, for if a demon she were tracking were to catch on too soon, it could put innocent bystanders at risk and her own life in jeopardy.

She opened the door and stepped out over a line of ash; part of a ritual she had performed to seal a barrier around her dwelling, this was a holy tradition taught by her clan that kept out demons, it allowed nothing evil to cross.

Sarain walked out into the fresh air, it was nearing dusk and the creatures would be out soon. She had enough time to get away from her quarters and into prime hunting grounds, usually the slums of the city. She would have to stay away from her place till dawn so that she couldn't be followed back.

Every night she hunted, trying to clean the streets of its vilest filth, but every day more demons seemed to crop up. Her work felt never-ending; she just hoped that she was making some sort of a difference.

Every now and then she heard a little rumor on the street about herself, more like an urban legend about a huntsman who executed evil doers. But being that there were rarely ever witnesses to her actions, the story didn't get around much, and her description had become widely altered, usually to that of a man who was seven feet tall and skillfully swift like a ninja. Sarain only stood at five feet and six inches, and while she was stealthy and quick, she did not fly about like a ninja. She wasn't sure where the male aspect came into the story; she figured that the tellers of the story must have thought that it would appear more plausible and accepting to be saved by a mysterious man than a strong woman.

Though one thing that the people usually did get right was the unusual violet eyes of their rescuer; an obvious shade of purple made her stand out from others. Most mistook it for color enhancing contacts, but Sarain's abnormal eye color was all natural. In her youth her clan had taken this as a sign of her being a savior to her people. Now she hid her eyes from the public, trying to not draw unwanted attention, she avoided eye contact. Those who did notice would either give her a double glance or a drunken comment like, "Whoa, cool contacts!" Sarain did not find this amusing, mostly since she was normally on a hunt and didn't want her presence announced. Not much could be done to conceal her eyes; contacts would be too much of a hassle and sunglasses would be a hindrance. Avoiding people and stares worked best.

Sarain didn't have to worry about any of that tonight. The streets were strangely clear, leaving her to walk freely; her hand always near her weapon. A quick draw of her blade was essential to her work; it made the difference of life and death for her and anyone she may be saving. Beheading would kill most demons, and a swift piercing of the heart would destroy nearly all half-demons.

These half-demons were internationally known as vil sangs or "Vile Blood." Both humans and demons view vil sangs as tainted blood creatures. More commonly known as vampires to society, vil sangs were formally humans who became infected by demonic blood from either a demon or another vil sang. However, against the popular beliefs, vil sangs are unable to turn into bats and do not sleep in coffins. The demonic blood does make them stronger and forever youthful, but vil sangs are weaker to sunlight than regular demons, and can be killed by it. They feed on human blood to sustain their own from the virus within, keeping them strong and energized. A vil sang that goes without blood would grow crazed and sickly, and although it wouldn't kill them to go bloodless, they would become more sensitive to light to the point that even artificial light could hurt them. Vil sangs look like regular people except when they're enraged; that's when their fangs descend and their eyes glow. The demon blood in them brings out the natural dark side in mankind, and over time can cause them to become more evil. Vil sangs made directly from demons usually take on more demonic features than just the glowing eyes and fangs. They are also stronger than a common vil sang; but most demons don't like to infect humans, since they despise vil sangs and would rather just make the kill.

It was dark now, no signs of a demon, and only a few people out. The lack of people could explain the lack of demons. While demons don't like crowds, they do like to pick off easy targets, such as people walking alone. Demons like to hunt humans for sport, and would often make trophies from their remains. They also would at times feed on humans, viewing any creature or animal as just meat.

Sarain didn't know if she should be glad or disappointed by the absence of demons. She felt that if she wasn't killing them, then that meant they were killing someone somewhere else. She knew she couldn't force them to come out, but she needed to feel as though she had a purpose, that her life had meaning.

A drunken couple walked out of a bar swaying toward her. Sarain moved away and lowered her eyes. The lady giggled, as if the man had told her a joke, as they passed her. Sarain went unnoticed.

She walked on down a darkened alley way. The only street light was broken; it had been for some time. The city didn't care about its slums and ghettos. She had come upon plenty of demons killing people, and often never heard anything about it in the news. The city didn't care, most cities she had lived in didn't care.

Shadows lurked all around. That's where they lived. Sarain watched for a moment, but didn't want to look too observant. Nothing, no movement. She kept on walking.

Hours went by making it very late in the evening. Not much longer before her patrol would be over. Inactive nights were rare, but were her goal, if she could lower the demon activity, then she would move to a new city, and start over again. This is what she did, how she lived.

Sarain turned onto another street, this one also dark. She thought she saw something scurry in the distance, but was unsure. A few steps more were followed by what sounded like a hiss. However, she couldn't be sure. But when she heard a yelp, she stepped up her pace. Someone was yelling in the distance; an attack was being made. The night wouldn't be inactive after all.

Upon closer investigation, Sarain discovered a boy struggling to get away from a coarse-looking demon. Its skin was like cracked desert ground, its eyes glowed green, and it swatted at the boy with fiercely long talons. The boy screamed; he had wedged himself in a small gap between buildings, one that the beast was too large to enter. Too preoccupied with the boy, the demon didn't see Sarain approaching behind it. She unsheathed her machete and began to raise it in the air. But when the boy saw her, he yelled out, "help", causing the creature to turn around to see who had arrived.

Sarain quickly ducked as the beast swung its large claw at her. It lunged toward her, knocking her against a wall. She held on to her knife, and forcefully shoved the monster back. While it was big, she nevertheless found the strength to fight it off. The creature swatted at her again, and missed once more. She sprung forward, and slashed her machete through the air, slicing off the demon's head. It fell limply to the ground with not even a twitch. It was dead.

Sarain wiped off her blade, and then put it back in its sheath. She gazed over at the boy, who cowered in his crawlspace. "You can come out now," she said, backing away from the boy's position.

He squeezed through, and stepped forward. He brushed himself off and stared down at the remains, and said, "What was that?"

"A demon," Sarain answered.

The boy's face went pale as he responded, "Seriously?" then paused and said, "How did you do that?"

"Training," she simply replied.

The boy glanced down again at the remains and said, "Are you just going to leave it there? What if someone finds it?"

"The daylight will take care of it." After a moment of silence, she asked, "Why are you out so late?"

"I'm old enough," the boy answered.

"What are you, like nine?" she asked.

"No, I'm eleven," he said sounding offended then shot back with, "What are you doing here?"

"Apparently saving you. Besides I'm twenty and able to take care of myself," she replied, and then repeated, "So, why are you out so late?"

"I was looking for my brother, Nate," he finally answered.

"Well you should wait for him at home," she firmly said.

"He's been gone for three days," the boy added.

Sarain sighed, it didn't look good, but she replied with, "Well then you should call the police."

"The police don't care; they just think he's a runaway. Besides, my brother is nineteen, he doesn't hit their list of importance," he responded.

"You should go home and let your parents handle it," Sarain said, not looking at the kid.

"I don't have parents, it's just me and my brother, there's no one else at home," he pleaded.

Sarain gazed over at the boy, and sighed again; she knew now that she would have to watch over him.

Chapter 2

After sun up, Sarain found herself in a small one bedroom apartment downtown. Following a few hours of conversation, she learned that the boy's name was Kit, and that his brother, Nate, had been taking care of him for the past two years since their mother's death, who had been mugged and murdered. Their father was a deadbeat and hadn't been in the picture for many years. Kit had always been able to rely on Nate, and didn't believe that he would abandon him. He had expected him home from work three nights earlier. At first when he didn't show, Kit had assumed that Nate had to pull a double shift. But by the next night, Kit had become worried. When he finally went to the police, they shrugged off the disappearance as just Nate trying to escape his responsibilities. They had tried to contact child services for Kit, but he took off from the station. Now he had resorted to looking for Nate on the streets.

In this time, Sarain had also taken it upon herself to seal a barrier around Kit's building. The ritual had taken most of the time, especially with Kit continuously asking questions. She eventually sent him inside to wait for her to finish.

Currently Sarain was back inside, having explained that the barrier kept out demons. She was waiting for Kit to bring her a picture of Nate. She had agreed to look for him, figuring that it was better than Kit going out and looking for Nate himself. He had agreed to stay safely in his apartment until she gave him some answers. Sarain understood that it was possible that there would be no answers, and if it came to that she would have to turn him over to child services. She knew that he wouldn't be able to take care of himself, and she couldn't take him in - her lifestyle couldn't fit a dependent in it nor did she want the responsibility that would come with him.

Kit came back with a picture; he seemed to cling to it, holding it near him. As he handed Sarain the photo, he said, "Sorry, this was the most recent picture I could find."

The picture was two years old; it was of him and Nate at a park, Nate had him in a headlock, but they both were smiling. It was taken by their mother.

"It'll do," she said, taking the photo. She saw Kit's look of concern, so she added, "It could be something else other than a demon, if that's what you're thinking. He could have been in an accident, it may sound bad, but he could just be resting in a hospital somewhere. Normal things do still happen."

Kit nodded and responded, "I just can't believe that monsters are real. Nate use to always call me a scaredy-cat for wanting to sleep with the light on when I was little."

"Well, only daylight would actually help you. A night light wouldn't do anything," Sarain commented, and then noticed that her remark wasn't helping him with his fears. She wasn't used to being sensitive to others' feelings; these were emotions she had long since lost.

She got up to leave, and Kit quickly asked, "Are you going?"

"I have to, if I'm going to find out anything on your brother," she glanced around for a moment then said, "Do you have enough food?"

"Yeah… Are you coming back?" Kit questioned, sounding like a scared child.

"I will when I find something," Sarain replied reassuringly. But she was only going to give it a couple of days before she would contact the authorities on Kit's situation. There wasn't much hope, and Kit needed stability. She would do what she could, but couldn't let herself get too drawn in. Her work was too important.

She departed, and as she was walking down the apartment stairs, she contemplated her next move. She would have to rest first, but aside from questioning random people and physically searching the streets for Nate, there wasn't much she could do. She didn't have the type of resources that the police would have when searching for someone. And she normally wasn't searching for humans. Besides, odds were that any news Sarain would have for Kit wouldn't be good.

After she slept, Sarain was once again walking the streets. She left her residence earlier this time, giving her a few more hours of daylight to survey people about Nate. She showed around his picture, but no one recognized him. She first tried more public crowded places, stores and such. When that didn't pan out, she tried the more slummy areas, seedy bars, and underground clubs; the people at these places were even more reluctant to talk.

Sarain stepped into another tavern; this one had puddles of liquid on the ground, which she hoped was alcohol, as soon as she walked in. The place smelled stale and was poorly lit. Some old sounding twangy music played on the radio while the patrons sat around lazily; most were overweight and looked dirty. She approached the bar, where the majority of the people were sitting, and as she got near she saw a cockroach run down the counter. She cringed, this place made her house seem like a palace.

The bartender glanced up at her and asked, "What can I get you, missy?"

"I'm not here for a drink. I'm looking for this man," Sarain replied holding up the photograph.

"I just serve, I don't watch," he answered back gruffly.

Sarain sighed and took a look around. A man sitting close by was staring at her and he waved her over; he looked rough, but was nothing compared to the demons she fought. She walked to his table with him checking her over as she approached.

"Who you searching for, honey?" the rough man asked.

Sarain held up the picture and replied, "This man, his name is Nate."

The man quickly glanced at the photo and said, "Who is he to you?"

Sarain stared at the man and answered, "A friend... He's missing and needed at home."

"It sounds like you could use a real man at home, honey. Why don't you sit your pretty little self down and let me buy you a drink," he boldly spoke, making her disgusted.

"Not interested. I just want to know if you've seen him," she stated, glaring back.

He shrugged, "Can't say I have... But it seems like a lot of people are going missing these days. Not really a bad thing though, news says that crime and gang activity is at a record low in the city. But then again, it's never safe for a sweet thing like you to be walking around alone."

"Well I manage just fine," she said firmly.

This method appeared pointless to Sarain. She would have to go about searching differently. She turned and headed for the door. When she reached the exit she heard the rough man call out sarcastically, "You be careful out there, honey!"

But Sarain wasn't the one who needed to be careful.

Stepping outside, Sarain discovered that the day had transformed into night. This was alright with her; she felt she worked better at night.

The streets were quiet, and thinking about it, they had been fairly empty of late. Sarain thought over what the rough man had said about people missing and crime being low. She had been ridding this city of its demons for a while now, but that wouldn't change the regular human crime level, like gangs, rapes, and muggings; that was all human. She wasn't sure about actual missing people, she hadn't been seeing any flyers or anything in the papers looking for people, but there was definitely less activity on the streets. This wasn't really her concern, and all in all, less crime was a good thing. Besides, fewer people hanging out on the streets also meant fewer people she'd have to save or that could get in the way of her work.

The moon shone down brightly and the air was cool. The vacant streets felt peaceful to Sarain, this wasn't a feeling she experienced frequently. She usually felt empty, not necessarily sad, but just lacking of emotion altogether. Yet she believed this made her a better hunter; if she didn't feel fear then her mind wouldn't get clouded with thoughts of worry and doubt.

The road was wet and appeared to shine under the light of the moon. Sarain's footsteps were soft on the concrete, she had learned to walk lightly so not to be heard. Trees nearby swayed in the wind, leaves rustled, and a cricket chirped. She could hear the music from a car driving in the distance, and people talking in the building to her right. She focused her hearing so that she could absorb all the sounds around her, and listened for anything out of the norm. The noise of her surroundings faded and somewhere out in the vastness ahead of her she could hear footsteps; they were walking away at a steady pace. They were definitely an alone pair, but they weren't necessarily demonic; she would have to investigate further. She picked up her speed to catch up to the source of the sounds.

The moon kept the street well lit, so Sarain walked in the shadow of the buildings to keep out of sight. Just ahead she could see the individual come into view. From this distance, the being looked human, but Sarain realized that if this was a vil sang then she wouldn't automatically be able to tell by looking. She picked up the pace, but still held back, she didn't want to bring attention to herself. From behind, the person looked male, with short hair and an athletic build. She couldn't see his face, and he also seemed to keep to the shadows. It was growing late in the evening, not too many people would be out at such an hour. This man could be an insomniac out for a walk, a thug searching for an opportunity, or something else altogether. Her gut told her to follow the man, something just felt strange about him. He didn't appear to be looking around; he walked as if on a path, and he didn't check streets signs either, so he must have known where he was and where he was going.

Sarain followed him for about a mile, all the while thinking that everything seemed too perfect; his straight steps on his course with him never looking around or back, and finding him on a night so quiet with empty streets. It almost felt like a trap, but to be so, she would have to assume this man was indeed a vil sang, who knew who she was and where she'd be, and this wasn't very likely. She was a better hunter than that, and kept a low profile purposely so that the demons would never see her coming.

They finally came upon his destination, a club called The Purge. It was one of those low key clubs; much like a rave, it was located in an old warehouse and didn't check IDs. It was in downtown slum central, and wasn't the kind of place for regular club-goers. Word on the street was that this club dealt heavily into drugs and alcohol, and was likely to have mob connections, because the police never touched it. Sarain had never been inside herself, being that she preferred to avoid crowds. Now it was beginning to look like her mysterious hiker was just another junkie looking for a fix. She started to rethink her pursuit on the man, when something suddenly caught her attention. The man had stepped into the light of the club sign, and once lit up, she realized that she had been trailing Nate all along. It was a lucky break that left Sarain feeling unsettled; she didn't like nor believed in coincidences.

Chapter 3

Sarain was surprised to find Nate so quickly, and she was amazed to find him alive. Most people who went missing in slums like these either turned up dead or didn't turn up at all.

She watched as Nate walked up and exchanged words with a large man standing in front of the entrance. After a moment, the large man disappeared inside the club while Nate waited outside. Sarain refrained from approaching him, and felt it best to hold back in the shadows and see how things played out. Nate kept his back to her as he waited. She wondered if he could be waiting for drugs. Kit had never mentioned Nate having a drug habit, but she figured that drugs would be something that Nate would most likely not want to share with his younger brother. She observed that he remained motionless, his head stayed straight forward, and he didn't seem interested in his surroundings. His behavior wasn't that of a junkie, he should be fidgety. But why else would he abandon his only family for a place like this?

A few minutes went by with no change until the large man returned followed by a tall blond man. The blond man was well dressed with well-kept chin length hair, his physical stature was toned, and Sarain got the impression that he was extremely into appearances. She also first and foremost noticed that the man was incredibly pale; this was something she watched out for in her line of work, however she couldn't make assumptions.

The blond man dismissed the large man, who went back to his original position at the door. The blond man then led Nate aside where they had a conversion, but it was mostly one sided with the blond man doing the majority of the talking. Sarain was unable to make out what the men were saying; with the distance and the noise coming from the club, eaves dropping was out of the question. She did watch intently, searching for any other sign besides paleness that might point to the blond man being a vil sang. But most of the time vil sangs only showed their demonic features when they were enraged and this blond man was staying composed.

They finished talking and the blond man quickly headed back inside. Nate soon after started walking off in the opposite direction, keeping on a steady path once again. Sarain considered following the blond man into the club to get a better look, and then remembered Kit. She had made him a promise, and understood that finding out what was going on with Nate had to come first. Even if it meant letting a possible vil sang slip through her fingers. And if he had been a vil sang she was curious to what business he had with Nate. Perhaps she wouldn't be bringing happy news to Kit after all. But this was taking place at a club, a public place, and a seedy crime-filled one at that; it was possible that everything could just be within regular human wickedness.

Sarain trailed after Nate, but kept distance between them. She wondered when she should approach him, and if she should do it in a populated area or not. Given the time, she was most likely not going to find a populated area. Probably for the best, because she knew what she might have to do. She thought about Kit at home waiting for her to return with information on his brother, and hoping that it would be good. She so wanted to be able to give him good news too; that's why she wished she hadn't gotten so involved in Kit's problem. It was better for her to not feel compassion, it only made her weak.

Sarain continued to follow Nate for another two miles before he finally came to a stop. He stood there, back to her, perfectly still, and staring up. Sarain recognized where she was, they were standing outside in a back alley behind Kit's apartment building. If Nate was a vil sang than he wouldn't be able to go inside thanks to the ritual she had performed around the building, and his just standing there didn't look good. She felt that now was the time to confront him. No one was around, and his journey had ended. She slowly approached him, but stopped short before getting too close.

"Nate," she called out softly to him.

He swiftly turned around, but it seemed as though he was reacting more to the noise than to his name. He stared at her blankly like a deer in headlights, unmoving.

"Nate," she called out again, "Are you okay?"

He didn't answer; he just stood there like he was unable to communicate. Sarain had never seen this before, whether he was a junkie or a vil sang he should have responded. He could be confused, and maybe suffering from a concussion.

"Nate, I'm a friend of your brother, Kit. He's been looking for you, he's worried," Sarain relayed, hoping to jog his memory.

"...Kit?" he repeated faintly.

"Yes, Kit, your brother," she said again.

She took a step closer to Nate, almost within arm's length, and then saw his eyes settle on her, but not her face. Was he looking at her neck, she quickly thought; no, he was staring at her necklace, her ankh cross.

Sarain gazed up into Nate's eyes, and saw the glowing tinge she hoped not to see. He was a vil sang, and she only had one thing left she could do. Her hand went to her machete and as if reading her mind, Nate hissed and lunged at her with his fangs starting to descend. Even with his demon speed, Nate couldn't out run Sarain; she rapidly dodged his attack, whipped out her blade, and lunged back at him full force. She felt her knife sink in, all the way to its hilt. A perfect hit directly to the heart.

The fire in Nate's eyes soon faded, he fell to the ground, landing on his back. He stared up at the apartment building, his eyes settling on a window, possibly Kit's. His eyes were just a normal brown now, and he looked like the guy in Kit's photo. A tear ran down Nate's cheek as his eyes glazed over.

It disturbed Sarain, how easy this all came to her. While Nate could only have been a newly born vil sang, it bothered her that her instincts were stronger than a beast's. But what was more troubling, was the fact that this was what she worried about, and not the bearing of bad news to Kit. Perhaps she was more detached from her emotions than she had earlier thought.

Sarain gazed down at Nate's lifeless body. If she hadn't known better she would have thought she was looking down at the corpse of a human. She couldn't fathom his bizarre behavior; why hadn't he just attacked her from the beginning? And why did he not seem to remember Kit at all? Sarain only knew the basics about vil sangs, she didn't know what went on in their heads, only that the demon blood inside made them turn blood thirsty and evil. But she had never seen a vil sang behave robotically before, and was curious to find out why.

Sarain stared up at Kit's building. She would have to tell him the grave news soon, but first, she needed to find out what Nate had wanted from the pale blond man back at the club. And if he too was a vil sang like she had previously suspected.

It wasn't long before Sarain was back in front of the club, The Purge. She watched from afar, debating if it would be best to just go right in; if she did, she could try to blend in, but there would be good odds that she'd be observed in whatever she did. She would have to be sneaky but come across casual in doing so. The large man was still guarding the door, and there was no way of seeing inside. The windows were all made with thick blurry tiled glass. Clubs were a popular place for vil sangs to inhabit, the drunken club-goers made easy targets; Sarain had tracked and killed many vil sangs from clubs. She didn't much like going inside them though, far too crowded for her taste. But tonight she would have to if she wanted to find out what had happened to Nate. She made up her mind, she was going in.

Sarain walked out from the shadows, and headed towards the club entrance. She approached the large man who stared onward, and towered over her in both height and size. She peered up at him when he didn't move or open the door.

"Are you going to let me in?" she asked straight forward and without politeness.

The large man glanced down at her and said, "No more entries tonight, we're near closing." He remained strong and steady, blocking the doorway.

Sarain sighed; she would apparently have no luck tonight. She turned around to leave and found the blond man standing in front of her. She didn't flinch, yet it caught her off guard, and thought it odd that she had never heard him drawing near. He was indeed very pale up close, and even now looked quite polished. He stood there with a smile, and Sarain noticed that his eyes were an unusually bright shade of blue, but they didn't glow; at least not at the moment.

"I see you finally decided to come in, too bad you're too late; closing hour," the blond man stated pompously.

"You were watching me?" Sarain asked with surprise.

"Well I saw you waiting there across the street looking toward the club. I didn't realize it took so much thought into coming in," he responded sounding smug.

Sarain's blade flashed into her mind, but it was still too soon to tell. Besides, she couldn't move on the man with his large guard so near.

"You probably should have come in earlier when you were watching me and my associate talk," the blond man said casually.

Sarain felt her heart stop for a second; she had known that she hadn't hidden well when she was contemplating going in the club, but she had been much further away and better concealed when she had observed him with Nate earlier.

"Are you alright? You look bewildered. I think it would be best for you to go home and get some rest," he spoke condescendingly.

Sarain collected herself and shot back, "I didn't ask for your opinion."

The man put his hands up as if to keep her at bay, and replied, "Just a simple suggestion," then extended a hand out to her and said, "The name is Winston, by the way."

Sarain simply stood there; she glanced at his hand, but made no attempt to shake it. Her expression was one that wasn't amused.

Winston moved his hand back, but then gestured to her and asked, "And your name is?"

She didn't reply, she only glared at him.

"Not very friendly, are you?" he remarked. His eyes then settled on her ankh. She noticed it too. She waited for a reaction, but he merely smiled, and said, "Nice necklace."

The entrance to the club abruptly opened, and Sarain's attention quickly went to behind her. The final club-goers were leaving, and were now crowding past her. She turned back toward Winston, but he was no longer there; he was nowhere in sight. She scanned the crowd with no luck; no sign of him. It looked like her new acquaintance hadn't stayed to finish the conversation, and she still had questions that needed to be answered.

Chapter 4

One steady footstep after another; it was quiet as the morning sun turned the dark sky just a slight shade of blue. Sarain hurried to reach her destination before time ran out. Dawn was approaching and she had one last thing she needed to do. She stopped and stood there waiting, gazing down on what was once a loving brother, and while she had never actually known him, she felt that it would be wrong to leave him alone. The sun would soon take care of her work; she normally would leave it at that, but today she required seeing it through. Countless times she had left the bodies of beasts to dissolve in the daylight, but this time, with this one, she could see the man it once was.

In her hand she held a picture; a happy family in a park, two brothers who would go to great lengths to protect the other. Kit would have no family now; no one to protect and no one to protect him. Sarain could try, but she was no real substitute, she lacked the instincts to care for someone. Both brothers had just been boys doing what came natural to them. She was the one who was unnatural, breaking the mold on what should have been a normal young woman. No, she had never been normal, she hadn't been lucky enough to experience that. She could only try her best, so that someone out there could live up to the standard that she couldn't. That's why she worked.

Sarain could feel the warmth of the sun on her back; she closed her eyes and let it embrace her. Its tenderness gave her a brief wave of tranquility, and it was almost as if being loved. When it past, she opened her eyes and saw nothing but ash, the deed was done. She gave what remained one last look, and departed to go finish her task; it was time to tell Kit.

Each step up a stair was one that Sarain didn't want to make. She didn't long to see the look on Kit's face when he heard the news. But she found herself climbing his apartment's stairs; the boy deserved to know. Once she reached his door, she paused for a moment; she could still turn back. And then she thought of her own family, something she rarely did, and closed her eyes, hoping to force her thoughts away. Kit was all she wanted to think about.

Sarain took a deep breath, and knocked on the door. She heard the creaking of footsteps on the other side quickly approaching. A chain rattled, and then the door slowly opened. Kit stood tiredly in the door way; he looked like a small child, and as though he hadn't slept in quite some time. He pushed the door open, without a word, to let Sarain in. She walked past him and he locked up. Afterward, she turned to him and waited for him to ask, "Is Nate alright?"

She had prepared herself for this instance, but suddenly couldn't find the words. Instead, she bit her lower lip and shook her head no. Kit began to cry, and Sarain knew that she didn't need to say anything now. She gazed down at the sobbing boy, his heart was breaking, but she couldn't comfort him. She watched him till he stopped crying. His tears were then replaced by a sorrowful silent expression on his face; Sarain recognized this look, it was the same one on her face the last time she was able to see her reflection, and it was a look she didn't wish to see again.

She handed him back the photo that he had loaned her. She worried that he would start to cry again, but he didn't. Kit sat down, and then stared blankly at the ground. He brought his hand to his face and wiped his tears away, and weakly said, "Who's going to take care of me now?"

Sarain thought of child services; Kit would be placed in a foster home, but would mostly likely never be adopted. He was too old, and from what she could tell, too rebellious. And now he had learned the streets cruelest lessons; his fate was beginning to look very similar to her own.

Sarain wanted to get back to her regular life and duties, but surprised even herself when she told Kit, "You can stay with me." The words had come out her mouth like breathing, and she realized that maybe she needed him as much as he needed her. Caring over him made her feel human.

He agreed with a simple "okay." She had him pack up his things, only what was essential, and she took from his apartment what she thought she would require for him. As they left, Kit gave his family's home one long last look good-bye; a lifetime of happy images, smells, and memories he would leave behind. He closed his eyes, and could see himself sitting to dinner with his mother and Nate, something that could never happen again. It was time to go.

Sarain didn't want Kit to turn into her, but she would have to teach him what he'd need to know to survive. She placed her hand on his back, and led him out the door. And as the door closed behind them, so did the chapter of Kit's childhood.

Nate's vacant eyes stared up at Sarain. His lips did not move, but she heard his voice say in a low raspy whisper, "I saw nothing." His broken body lay at her feet; she may have been the one who killed him, but she wasn't what destroyed him. She never saw true life in his eyes, not even behind the fiery glow when he tried to kill her. Something stole his essence before he became a monster. Where had he been those three days he was missing? He had seemed to be on a mission when she had interrupted him. He may have been coming after Kit, possibly to severe his ties to humanity; it wouldn't have been the first time she saw it happen. But his eyes, so lifeless, so without passion; vil sangs normally had such a lust for blood burning through them that it kept them lively: Except Nate had been more like a beaten dog, and Sarain had been humane enough to put him out of his misery. Still, in his last moment, she had thought she spied one final glimmer of the man he had been in that single tear he shed. Or at least that was what she wanted to believe.

His words "I saw nothing" rang through her head. What did they mean?

Wait, he never said that; she must be dreaming again.

Sarain sat up in bed and realized that the deceased were speaking to her in her dreams again.

It was nearing dusk before Sarain finally dragged herself out of bed. The events from the previous night didn't weigh her down like she thought they would; she actually felt fairly like her normal self. She went over her mental checklist on what she would need to do tonight; she would have to first make sure Kit was okay, then she needed to go to The Purge to find out what she could on Winston, and see what his connection to Nate was. She had to find this out before she could corner him, she couldn't afford to make any mistakes. She probably wouldn't be getting to any of her regular hunting tonight, which bothered her a bit; she liked to feel that she was making a difference, and to feel that, she preferred the instant gratification of a kill. However, if all goes well with her pursuit, she may still get her kill.

Sarain dressed, and walked quietly into her den. Kit was still sleeping in his sleeping bag on the floor, which he had laid against the wall. He clung to his pillow like a small child would a teddy bear; he had fallen asleep soon after his arrival. He slept deeply, but let out an occasional whimper throughout the night. She didn't want to wake him from his much needed rest.

She made herself a simple meal of scrambled eggs and toast, but this time she made extra in case Kit got hungry, and sure enough the smell of the food woke him. He stretched up with a yawn and rubbed his eyes, when he saw the food he promptly got up and made himself a plate. He shoveled the eggs into his mouth hungrily, and then crammed in two pieces of toast to follow. Sarain poured him a glass of milk to wash it all down; seeing his appetite she grasped that she would have to start getting much more food from now on.

She finished her meal and turned to Kit, who was still stuffing his face. When he saw her staring he slowed down and curiously asked, "What?"

"I have to go work," she told him.

"Are you going to go kill demons?" he questioned, sounding both excited and scared.

"Yes, maybe, but I'll be safe about it," Sarain answered, noting his concern.

Kit gave her a somewhat puppy dog face and replied, "Okay."

She got up, and did a quick scan of the room before she said, "You should have everything you need here. Don't leave the house, there's a barrier around it. I should be back after dawn."

Kit nodded, and then went back to eating. Sarain was surprised to see how well he was doing. Perhaps she wouldn't have to worry about him so much after all.

Chapter 5

With Sarain all geared up, she left the house moving hastily; she had gotten a late start and needed to move faster so that her scent would be away from her dwelling by nightfall. She also had to get downtown to the club on foot, and even with her speed, it would take a while. She went everywhere on foot, a car was too pricy and too easy to track. In addition, it would limit where she could go and was too noticeable when following someone or something. It would also be an inconvenience to have to continuously go back to a car if she left it to go on foot. When she left cities, she'd pack up what few things she had, and take a bus to her next destination.

Sarain still had to figure out if she should keep Kit in school; she had never been to a traditional school herself, being part of a nomadic clan. She had been home schooled and then later self-taught. She could try and teach Kit; she most likely had to if she were to keep moving from city to city. She wasn't sure if she was ready to be a parent, if that was what she would be; she figured herself more as a teacher, like what she had grown up with.

Sarain looked up at the sky; the clouds blocked the moon tonight, just a glimpse here and there between them. A gentle breeze picked up, the wind felt good against her skin, soft through her hair. She wasn't one for touching people; she didn't crave physical contact like so many other people do. It could have been because of her line of work; seeing evil and cruelty on such a regular basis didn't leave you longing to be touched. But she also could never understand why people felt the need to paw at one another; she thought it distasteful, especially in times when no love was involved. The caress of the cool night air was enough for her.

After a long trek and a lot of time to think, Sarain finally came upon The Purge. It was already open and the large guard was once again standing at the door. She didn't bother to wait and contemplate going in tonight, not after having been spied by Winston previously. She marched straight up to the entrance, and this time when the guard glanced at her it was followed by him opening the door for her. His eyes gave the impression that he recognized her from the night before, but he didn't say anything nor did his face make an expression. Sarain decided to pay no mind to the guard. She would worry later whether or not to check him out, but her vibes told her that he was human. There wasn't a particular thing that stood out about him as being human, but just a feeling that she had. She moved past him and went inside.

Inside the warehouse-turned-club was fairly crowded, but with the vaulted ceiling and the size itself, it was rather spacious. The dance floor was huge, and looked so shiny that it was almost reflective. It also had a cage with dancers at each corner. The lighting was dim, but colorful; the track lighting seemed to be on a twinkling-like setting, similar to Christmas tree lights. At one end of the club was a large bar with many bartenders and on the wall behind them was a hefty stock of alcohol. The music was some techno beat unknown to Sarain, and it blasted so loudly that you could barely hear anything else. Most people there were intoxicated, dancing wildly, and the majority of the women were dressed in revealing clothing despite it being a slightly colder night. Sarain herself didn't wear her trench coat that night; it would have made her stand out far too much. This meant she had to bring a much smaller knife, a switch blade, over her machete. She wore a plain fitted black long sleeve shirt with charcoal gray jeans with her long black wavy hair hanging freely; she undoubtedly was a lot more conservatively dressed than the other women there, but she didn't care, she looked casual enough to blend in and not sexy enough to stand out.

Sarain made her way through the room; with the crowd and the noise it would be hard for her to find out any information on this puzzling Winston character. She had to learn his connection to Nate and if he too was a vil sang, perhaps even the beast that turned Nate. So far there was no sign of him, but his behavior the night before with the guard made it seem as though he was there often. Her eyes searched over the faces on the dance floor, but didn't see his.

There had to be a better way of doing this, the thought occurred to Sarain. She had his name; if he truly was a regular, then others there might know him.

She moved towards the bar, and sat at an empty stool. She waited for a bartender to become free. Who better to recognize a regular than someone who worked there, but every employee stayed steadily busy. Sarain got up, leaned over the counter to be heard, concentrated her attention on one of the female bartenders, and said, "Can you help me? I'm looking for a man."

The bartender shook her head and replied, "Lady, I'm too busy to deal with your personal issues," and continued to take customers' orders.

Sarain sat back in her seat and sighed, then heard a chuckle to her right. She turned to see the culprit and saw the half drunken woman sitting next to her staring back at her. The woman's makeup was runny from sweat and her eyes looked glazy, she wore a flashy silver dress that Sarain thought was way too short. She smiled at Sarain and remarked, "Aren't we all looking for a man?"

Sarain realized that the woman misunderstood her; she quickly rectified the mistake and responded, "I'm actually looking for someone in particular."

"Who you lookin' for, I'm here a lot, I might know him?" the woman asked with curiosity.

"I'm looking for a blond man named Winston," Sarain answered hoping to finally have some luck.

The woman nodded and said, "Yeah, I've seen him around, but you don't want him. I hear he hangs out at that sleazy Velvet Rose place up north, you know, that whore house."

"How did you find this out," Sarain questioned, trying to figure out how reliable her tip was.

"Well, I have to admit, he is a hottie with those pretty eyes of his. I asked a girlfriend of mine who knew a guy who sometimes hung with him, what he was into, and she said he said that your Winston friend, strictly liked to keep things impersonal, and liked to go to the Velvet Rose to get his jollies off," the woman replied like a gossiping schoolgirl, then added, "It's a shame, he really is gorgeous."

"Yup, a shame," Sarain repeated in a sarcastic manner that was meant for only herself to understand. The tip didn't look very dependable, but Sarain didn't have anything else to go on. It couldn't hurt to check it out; Winston didn't appear to be at the club anyway.

Sarain thanked the woman, and left the bar. She made her way back through the crowd heading to the entrance, and thought how extremely un-thrilled she was about checking out a brothel; she couldn't possibly picture a great outcome there. Either she was dealing with a perverted man, or a vil sang... who may also be a pervert.

Sarain found herself on yet another long trek, this time heading north to the ill-famed Velvet Rose. She had heard of it before, even killed a demon or two in its area. It was another one of those places that the cops never seemed to shut down. The crime-lords of this city ran most of the big businesses, Sarain didn't like it, but she also didn't bother with human transgressions, so just let things be.

She plotted while she hiked; she couldn't just go busting into the Velvet Rose, their customers were typically men, and she couldn't pretend to work there or want to work there, because that would be too weak of a cover, and probably wouldn't work. She thought she remembered seeing a balcony window on the third floor; it stood out in her mind because it was the only window that hadn't been bricked up. She could try getting in through there.

Sarain's thoughts wandered back to the drunken woman at The Purge, fawning over how attractive she thought Winston was; Sarain hadn't even noticed; she had stopped observing people's attractiveness a long time ago. She had picked up on his arrogance though; it was a behavior she had always despised in individuals, especially in those who had no real value in character.

While thinking, Sarain realized that she really had never exchanged much conversation with a vil sang before, apart from whatever she needed to determine a person's status, whether it was demonic or not. But aside from that, she didn't know too much about a vil sang's behavior; all she really needed to know was that they killed humans, so she killed them. Although, she was beginning to wonder how much of their human personality they kept after becoming a vil sang.

The night was growing late, and Sarain could smell the scent of rain in the air; a storm was coming. The clouds lowly rumbled above and it began to sprinkle. She picked up speed, rushing to reach the Velvet Rose before the storm came down in its fullness. She weaved down streets and through alleys, whichever way would get her there faster. She raced, running at incredible speed, with the droplets of rain getting heavier. The Velvet Rose was just ahead; Sarain stopped and crept up, staying against the side of a building in the shadows. She would not let herself be seen this time, she needed to be able to catch Winston in his natural routine, and she didn't want him to see her coming. She slinked towards the building and was soon standing beside it staring up at the balcony window she remembered. It was indeed three stories up, and there wasn't a dumpster or trashcan around to stand on.

This might be more difficult than previously estimated, Sarain pondered. Her eyes then settled on the building next to it, it was close enough to use. The buildings were only five feet apart making it a small alley way. She looked up, the neighboring building was too high to safely jump from, but she still had another way. She pressed her back against the wall of the Velvet Rose, then bent her knee and put her right foot against it as well. With a deep breath to prepare herself, she quickly kicked off and lunged herself at the other building, twisting her body mid-way. Her feet hit it and kicked off again, pushing her upward. She spun her body around, and her feet hit the Velvet Rose, she jolted off again, and again, and once more; each sending her shooting upward till she finally leaped onto the balcony.

Sarain's heart raced from adrenaline, she took a moment to calm herself, and then peered through the lacy curtain on the other side of the glass. The room was dark, but the door was open and a light was on down the hall. The coast looked clear, now she only had to get inside.

Lightning flashed with a booming crack, the rain poured down stronger now, and Sarain got the idea that perhaps she could mask the sound of breaking glass by hitting the window when the thunder banged. She would have to kick in the window, running the risk of injuring herself since she didn't have her machete to bash it in with. Then an epiphany came to her, she tried the handle and the door slid open. She figured that the occupants would assume that no one would be able to get up to a third story balcony, so then they wouldn't worry about locking it.

She stepped inside, walking lightly so not to make the floor creak. She reached the door and peeked out into the hall; it was empty. She wondered how she would find Winston, if he was even there; she would have to search room by room. There were two other doors on this floor, she slowly crept to the first one, and noticed that the door was fitted with an old fashioned key lock, which meant a keyhole.

Sarain could hear someone shuffling from inside the room; she brought her eye down to the keyhole and peered through it. Two women were entertaining a short bald man, who definitely wasn't Winston. She turned her head away, she had seen enough. She moved to the next door, it stood ajar, and upon inspection she found that it was empty. She moved to the staircase; she had to be careful, wooden staircases were notorious for creaking upon stepping. Another deep breath before going, then she swiftly sprinted down the stairs, barely touching and staying on a single step. The stairs had slightly groaned, but not one real cracking sound.

The second floor hallway started around the corner from the stairwell. Sarain listened first to see if she could hear anyone moving down the hallway. The sound of high heels were retreating away from her direction, she heard a door squeak open and then a soft thud afterwards. She waited a bit; it was quiet, so she checked around the corner, down the hall. Empty, the coast was clear.

This hallway also had doors to three rooms; the first room was dark and vacant. She crept to the next room, the door was closed and light shined through the keyhole. She hesitated to look after her last act of voyeurism, but decided that she had to and gazed through. A young woman was inside with a middle-aged man, the woman was dressed up in a schoolgirl uniform and spanking the man with a ruler. Sarain saw something sparkle and realized that the man was wearing a wedding band. She found this more disturbing than what they were actually doing. She closed her eyes before things got graphic, and moved away from the door. While she knew that she wasn't the one being betrayed by the man, she still felt the feeling of hate rising in the pit of her stomach. In her line of work she saw beasts in many shapes and forms, and though this man may not be demonic, he was still just another monster to her.

Sarain moved on to the last door on the floor. The door was slightly open, just a crack, and candlelight flickered from inside. As she approached, she heard a woman moan. She braced herself for any explicit act she may see next. She reached the door and glanced in. The room was mostly dark; the few candles didn't give off much light. The forms of a man and woman were entwined on the bed; they were moving to rhythm and seemed too engrossed to notice Sarain peeking through the doorway.

The man started kissing the woman's neck, and Sarain began to move on from the door. Then something caught her eye; a sudden glimpse of blue. She stopped, and looked again. The man was Winston, but more importantly, the blue was from his brightly colored eyes, which Sarain probably wouldn't have seen in the dark if it wasn't for the fact that they were glowing. He bit into the woman's neck, but continued to move his body with hers. Winston was without a doubt a vil sang, however Sarain hesitated to attack. The woman appeared fine, she was still alive, and didn't seem startled by the blood sucking act. The woman was a willing participant, and had to be human because her eyes did not illuminate. Winston removed his fangs from the woman's throat, and then kissed her again. She put her hands on his back and tried to pull him down to her. He leaned in, and then looked up at Sarain.

Sarain's body went cold as she met his icy stare. His eyes glowed with passion; he gazed at her without expression, his mouth still smudged with blood. She didn't look away, and he kept his eyes on her. The other woman didn't appear to notice, she was too enthralled in the act to realize that Winston's attention was elsewhere. Sarain's hand tightened around her knife; she didn't want him looking at her, but he remained staring. Finally the woman brought her hands up to Winston's face and pulled him down for a kiss, breaking his gaze. When he broke from the woman's lips, his eyes went back to the doorway, but Sarain was gone.

Chapter 6

The sun shined down brightly, from the rich blue sky, upon a lavish green field. The field blossomed with wild flowers; colors of every kind could be seen by the eye. A small bright-eyed child wandered about, picking flowers to make a crown for her head. Her dress grazed against the grass as she skipped along. Her mother sat nearby, keeping ever watchful.

The girl plucked her last flower, its soft white petals brushed her skin. She added it to her already large collection. Entwining the stems, she weaved her crown, and placed it on her head; now she wore all the colors. She decided that she was fit to be a princess. If she were in a fairytale, then she would be ready to go to the ball, and in her mind, she was. She danced, twirling her dress and letting her dark waves of hair spin around her. Her dance partner, a monarch butterfly, fluttered above her, obviously attracted to the flowers.

The mother watched her carefree spirited child play. The girl was very happy and innocent, what a mother would want for her child. Though she knew that she wouldn't be able to shield her daughter from the cruelties of the world forever, she was glad that she could have peace for now.

After a while of swirling, the girl began to grow dizzy. She stumbled, swayed, and then came crashing down. The weight of her body fell onto one knee. The knee hit the ground hard and scraped open. Warm red blood flowed out from the wound, it stung and throbbed. The girl grabbed at her knee and called out, "Mama!"

It wasn't long before her mother was by her side. She calmed the girl, wiping away her tears, and moved her daughter's hand so that she could see the injury. It still bled. The mother put her hand on the wound, and closed her eyes. The knee grew warm, and the girl stopped crying. The mother then opened her eyes and removed her hand. The scrape was gone, the skin was unharmed. She then bent down and kissed her daughter's knee.

"Look, all better," the mother said.

The girl smiled up at her, her violet eyes bright once again.

"Sarain… Sarain are you awake?"

Sarain opened her eyes to see Kit looking back at her. She groaned. She was still tired from her overly intensive night before. She looked at Kit and saw the stressed expression on his face. She sighed and sat up. "What's wrong?" she asked him.

"I had a bad dream," he replied weakly.

"What was it about?" she said, trying to be sympathetic.

Kit crawled up on her bed like a frightened child and relayed, "I dreamt that my family was in the park and a demon came out of the sky and started hurting my mom. Nate tried to save her, but the demon killed him. My mom kept screaming for me to help her, but I couldn't move. Then she started saying that it was all my fault, and that she wished the demon had killed me instead."

"Your mom would have never thought that. You know better," Sarain stated.

"Yeah, I know... But it felt so real. And I still feel helpless," Kit whined.

Sarain contemplated for a moment, and then came up with a grand gesture. Her hands reached for her neck, and she felt for chain. She took off her ankh, and said to Kit, "I also lost my mom at a young age, but before she died, she gave me this. It's been in my family for generations; it protects you from evil things. And I want you to have it."

She put the necklace on Kit, he admired it for a second before saying; "I'm never going to take this off."

Sarain smiled, and replied, "Good, because we're family now."

Later that same day, once Sarain felt rested, she awoke and tended to Kit. She fixed him a meal and made sure that he was feeling better from his disturbing dream. He seemed well as they sat to breakfast; she was amazed at his ability to bounce back.

They ate their food in silence until Kit spoke up with a mouthful of food and asked, "What do you do when you go out hunting?"

"Well, you saw when I rescued you," Sarain answered briefly.

"Yeah, but is it always like that?" he continued to push.

Sarain sighed - she didn't want to disturb him with details - and responded, "Not always, I usually have to take some time to find them first. They hide a lot of the time. They normally like to stay in dark, unpopulated places."

"But do they sometimes go in crowds?" he pressed on.

"The ones that look human do, and they will eventually try to get a person alone somewhere," she replied.

"How can you tell when they are a demon or a real person?" Kit asked.

"When they get provoked their eyes glow and their fangs come out," she simply said.

"Do they ever still act human?" he curiously wondered.

Sarain thought for a moment, the question was one that rarely ever entered her mind, then she answered, "They pretend to, but they are still monsters."

Kit continued to eat again, and it was silent for a little while. He didn't talk until he finished his meal, and then just went on about mean kids in school that he thought were demons. So she explained that the demons also couldn't go out in sunlight, hence why she only hunted them at night. She also told him a few basic things about demons, like their weakness and how to hurt them.

While Sarain was cleaning up the dishes, Kit made another inquiry, "So what did you do last night?"

She stopped in place, and the image of Winston's blue glowing eyes staring through her flashed into her mind. A chill went down her back, and she shook the thought away, then answered, "I went to a club looking for the vil sang type of demons."

"Did you find any?" he asked with excitement.

"I found one," she replied.

"Did you get him?" he said like a child.

Sarain hesitated from the memory then said, "I will."

Kit responded with an ordinary "good" then went to his sleeping bag where he opened up a comic book and began to read. Nothing appeared to hold his interest long.

Sarain turned back to the dishes, and when she was almost finished she heard Kit ask, "Are clubs fun?"

"Some people think they are," she answered.

"Yeah, Nate liked clubs. He liked them so much that he worked at one," he said still staring at his comic.

This got Sarain's attention. She hadn't been sure where and how Nate had ended up a vil sang. She tried her best to keep her tone casual when she asked, "Really, what club did he work at?"

Kit didn't seem to notice Sarain's heightened interest, he just answered, "It had a funny name, I remember, because it reminded me of a cat; The Purr-ge. I don't know what it means, but he only worked there a couple of months."

"It means 'to rid of impurities'," she said realizing that that was the tie that fit Nate to Winston - they both frequented the club. It all could have been just a case of bad luck for Nate, but thinking about their interactions that first night and how the guard even went in to retrieve Winston, started to lead Sarain to believe that Winston may be more than just a frequent visitor of The Purge. She knew now that this wouldn't be a simple kill, she would have to go back and investigate further. But it was beginning to look like more might be taking place at this club than she had previously thought. And maybe the reason why the police never touched the place wasn't for the motives she had believed it was. Perhaps it was out of fear and not just human crime life.

Nearing nightfall, Sarain quickly dressed in her street clothes, simple all black once again, and readied herself to go off to the club. She checked on Kit first, made sure he had everything he needed, and told him not to leave the house.

She faced another long hike, though this time the sky was clear, so she wouldn't be burdened by rain. The moon was partly shadowed, so not much light lit the streets, but Sarain knew the way well. As she walked she pondered why Nate had stopped to talk to Winston that fateful night; it was something she constantly questioned in her head. Vil sangs normally don't stick around after they've turned another, not unless it was someone they had been close to in life, and all she could see that connected Nate and Winston was the club. And better yet, why turn Nate at all? Why not just kill him, and why him and not the woman at the Velvet Rose? Sarain couldn't make sense of it, but she aimed to find out.

When she finally neared the club the streets had become active, it appeared to be quite a busy night. Cars sped by looking for parking, and a large crowd of people waited outside the Purge's club doors. The club was already open, but was nearing full capacity, allowing only a few to enter. It would be a long wait if Sarain wanted to get in. She looked at the lengthy line, and debated if it was worth her time tonight; she could always try again another day, and do her regular hunting in the meantime.

She started to turn and leave when she heard someone call out, "Hey, you there!" People normally didn't address her, but Sarain looked up anyway to see what the commotion was. The large guard who had watched over the door every night that Sarain had been there was now looking at her from his regular position.

"You, Miss," he said still staring in her direction, "the boss has asked to let you right in."

"The boss?" she thought to herself. Was he talking about Winston? She hesitated for a second, she didn't like where this was going. She felt like a pawn in a game, but she had no other choice if she wanted to get to the bottom of this mystery. She wanted to give Kit an answer to why this all happened someday, something she had never obtained for herself. She just hoped to not get herself killed in the process.

Sarain reluctantly went inside.

Chapter 7

It was darker in the club tonight with an ever pulsating strobe light giving flash images of contorting dancers. The room was much more crowded than the night before; Sarain had to shove to walk through it. This wasn't going to be easy; with the room darker than before it left most faces in the shadows. She had lucked out last time by finding the drunken woman who had tipped her off about the Velvet Rose; Sarain didn't expect to be that lucky again. At least she knew to ask about the club's boss, but it wouldn't do her much good if she couldn't be heard over the blaring music. Besides, the employees had been too busy and reluctant to answer her before when the club was less crowded. But it looked as though Winston wanted her there, if he had asked to have the guard show her in. Perhaps she could use this to her advantage.

Sarain squeezed in between a lot of cluttered bodies; she needed to find a clearing. While trying to get by she felt a pair of strong hands wrap around her waist. She quickly spun around ready to hit the culprit, but came face to face with a mere intoxicated club-goer. It was a tall thin man with dark spiky hair and a lot of facial piercings. His eyes looked glazed over like he was possibly high or had one too many drinks. He didn't seem to mean her any harm, he just wanted a dance. Sarain shook her head at him and said "No", but the man didn't let go. She tried to shove him off, but with little room and his tight grip on her, she was unsuccessful in doing so. After about a minute of struggling with the man, Sarain saw another pair of arms move in between them. The new person pushed them apart, and got the spiky headed offender to back off. It was dark, and the moving lights were making it even harder to see, but she caught a glimpse of blond hair. Winston? The spiky haired man walked off, and Sarain's rescuer turned around. A familiar pair of blue eyes met hers. Yes, it was Winston.

She backed away bumping into a couple. She knew she needed answers, but she didn't feel right about being there; it didn't feel safe. She turned and pushed her way through the crowd. She needed to leave, she had to leave now. She could feel herself panicking, which she normally didn't do, but all her instincts were telling her to get out of there. She searched for the exit; she had gotten turned around in the dark crowd. She moved past a group of badly dancing girls, and met with a wall. She had gone the wrong way, she was at the back of the club, and the exit was on the other side.

Sarain made her way back through the crowd, she now knew where the exit was, but the room was quite large and the crowd was unbearably hard to move through. She pushed past another couple, and looked up to see how far from the exit she was. She suddenly stopped in her tracks. Winston stood before her. Her heart raced as she watched him take a step closer to her, but she held her ground.

"Leaving so soon?" he asked, sounding perfectly passive, then he added, "You know, the polite thing to do would have been to say 'thank you' after I helped you out back there, but running away, well that was very rude."

"I don't like to keep company with vil sangs," Sarain abruptly said.

"Then why did you come here?" Winston stated, and then continued by saying, "For someone who is so eager to get away, you sure like to seek me out."

"Don't flatter yourself, it's my job," she coldly responded.

He studied her for a moment, and finally said, "That's a funny job for a small girl such as yourself. I would think that if you were any good I would have heard of you. But I have never even heard so much as a name."

"My name doesn't matter, trust me. I'm good, that's why you haven't heard of me," Sarain shot back,

"Seems to me that if you were good, you would have killed me last night, instead of watching me with those unusual eyes of yours," Winston replied observantly.

"The girl was in the way," she said, half to convince herself.

"The girl was meaningless, you just liked what you saw," he arrogantly boasted.

"Don't make me sick, you're just another piece of filth that needs to be done away with. I just needed to find out what your motives were," Sarain snapped at him, but still tried to keep her voice down.

"If it made you so sick, why didn't you look away?" he pointed out calmly.

"Why didn't you just kill the girl?" she questioned, ignoring his comment.

"And what would be the point of piling up bodies, if I have willing participants at my beck and call? People like that don't just grow on trees, and it keeps me fed and overzealous hunters such as yourself off my back," Winston remarked making sense, but then he added in spite, "Besides, it's not like I don't enjoy a good kill, it's just smart business."

"You think you're so clever, then what's to stop me from killing you right now?" Sarain more calmly demanded.

"With this big crowd to witness?" he asked making another point.

"It's dark, people are drunk, and no one is even the slightest bit interested in what we are doing now. They may not even notice, and even if they did, there's no way they'd get a very good description of me," she stated with ease.

"Maybe, but do you really think I'm the only vil sang here?" he securely commented.

Sarain went cold; she had been too distracted to realize that he might not be alone. Of course, if he was the boss there, he surely would have other vil sangs on staff. They may not all be, but either way it would be too hard to easily tell.

"It's too hard for you to tell isn't it? Who in this mass is human and who isn't?" Winston observed.

Sarain looked out into the dancing crowd, the lights did flash and move wildly, but even with the abnormal lighting she still noticed quick glimpses of glowing eyes sporadically in the crowd. A glow that couldn't be explained by a mere reflection of light; she could tell the difference.

The dancers moved like flickering flames; each twisting rhythmically in the pulsating light. The crowd of club goers made a ring of fire around Sarain and her unholy companion, but this blaze wouldn't bring her or the half demon to his end, instead it kept them in a stalemate; each having to keep their attack on hold. Too many onlookers made it unsafe for either player to make a move. To the room they were just mere people having a minor disagreement, but in truth they were enemies that would kill the other upon the first real opportunity.

Winston smiled slyly. He knew he was safe; with the protection of his guards and the crowd, Sarain couldn't touch him. Though she could wait until dawn so he couldn't touch her, this still felt like a win for him.

She could see the demonic glow in his vibrant blue eyes, that glow they have when they make a kill. She knew his smugness, and wished so much to be able to wipe it off his face. She felt almost as if her own violet eyes were glowing. Her hand was to her side, on her switchblade, but she was unable to draw it. All Sarain could do was stare on.

Winston smiled once more and said, "It looks as though you are trapped."

"For now, but not forever," Sarain answered, her hand still on her weapon.

"But still, you are unable to move, and 'for now' is all I need to be pleased," he responded.

That's when suddenly something unforeseen to Sarain happened. Winston moved toward her; and with all her years of experience, she never would have estimated such a move. Winston had boldly grabbed her by the neck and pulled her to him. Before she could realize what had just taken place, she found herself lip locked with the deviant being. His lips were cold; not like ice, but more like trying to kiss a cool breeze. Neither had closed their eyes, and both stared at each other with a deadly gaze.

Why had Winston made such an unexpected move? Maybe just to rub his arrogance that much more into Sarain's face?   If so he had succeeded. Never had Sarain been so angered by a single act.

She shoved him away in disgust with him laughing instantly. He knew how much this behavior had disturbed her; being touched in such a way by something so unclean. Her hand went to her mouth as though it were missing. She tried to rub it clean, but it was no use; it now felt tainted.

Sarain backed away from Winston with him still laughing at her. She let herself get lost in the crowd. Yes, maybe some of them were vil sangs, but others were people, and anyone or anything was better company than a fiendish violator such as Winston. The other demons wouldn't care to toy with Sarain, they would just make a simple kill of her, but Winston's games were far crueler.

She waited amongst the dancers. She could no longer see Winston, but she felt his eyes still on her. She waited for hours, always feeling watched, until the club let out for closing hour, just before dawn. She slipped out with the crowd, and quickly made haste away from the club. She lingered a few blocks away, and made sure she hadn't been followed. It looked clear, but Sarain waited until sunrise before she headed back to her domicile.

This was the worst defeat Sarain had ever faced. She had lost innocent bystanders before, having been too late to save them, but she had never let a demon get the upper hand on her. And never had one gone through such great lengths to defile her. It was like Winston wanted her to come after him.

Chapter .8

A young girl, barely thirteen, stirred in bed. There was a commotion outside that woke her from her peaceful slumber. The room was dark, it was still night. She looked to the other side of the hut, where her grandfather slept, and saw that his bed was empty. She heard screams coming from nearby, and immediately shot up in bed. She went to the doorway, and held back the cloth curtain that covered the entrance. She could see fire in the distance; a man she recognized as a teacher came running from its direction yelling, "They've broken through the barriers! They're coming in hordes!"

The girl had no idea who the teacher was talking about, but he was usually a calm and collected man, and now he had been reduced to a blathering imbecile. More familiar faces came running from the fire, all looking just as frightened. She watched as they all ran past her hut, some of them carrying small children that weren't from their families. She stepped out to get a better look of things, and saw men marching in the distance, coming from the fire. The fire was blazing high and had somehow turned blue. These were not men she recognized, and they held weapons in their hands. As they grew closer, she noticed something else peculiar about them, their eyes glowed.

She knew what they were, they weren't men at all; they were vil sangs. She knew all about demons, and how to destroy them. The sun wouldn't rise for hours, and would be no help to them. They would have to dismember or destroy the heart of each and every beast. Their numbers were great, but they were the weakest of all the demon types; if her clan were to survive a horde of any type of demons, these were the likeliest kind to beat.

She saw men from her clan coming back with weapons in their hands; axes, blades, and spears, all preparing to do battle. Some women and children still ran by. The vil sangs were growing near. The girl stood still in her place, frightened by the overwhelming sight, until a familiar voice shouted out, "Sarain!"

She turned and saw her grandfather racing toward her. He scooped her up in his arms and carried her away from the chaos. He didn't take her far, but he took her to a clearing out of view. He looked around and saw a pile of crates the clan used when moving to carry produce. He took the lid off one and placed her inside.

Sarain crouched down while asking, "Why are you putting me here?"

He gave another quick glance around and said, "You have to hide. The others don't realize that you can't out run these beasts. Staying put is your best chance."

"What about you?" she asked with worry.

"I'm not exactly hiding size, besides, I need to fight. I probably have more experience than anyone else here," he told her. He picked up the crate lid and placed it on, and told her, "Try not to make a sound, and don't come out until sunrise."

"Yes, sir," she shakily said from inside. Sarain watched through the cracks between the panels of wood on the crate as her grandfather picked up a spare blade someone had left behind, and headed back towards the battle.

She was left alone to hear shouting and clangs from metal nearby. The sounds were getting closer. Eventually she saw people moving into the clearing; the battle was coming nearer.

A boy named Orran, who was only a few years older than Sarain and whom she considered a friend, held a sword preparing to fight the vil sangs off. Other men, most of them grown, also stood with Orran waiting for the assault. Soon the demons flooded in. The vil sangs moved faster than men, they flipped and sliced their blades wildly through the air. Many men fell early on, bodies slashed to bits. But a few held their ground, one being Orran. Though he was young, he fought well, having trained immensely; he was the top in his class. Sarain had sparred with him a few times, but he always took it easy on her even though she would be trying her best to beat him. She suspected that he knew she liked him although she put great effort into hiding it. She watched as he swung his sword with great force, slicing away at vil sangs. He thrust the blade through the chest of one, and it dropped dead before him. Slowly but surely the vil sangs numbers dwindled. Survival was looking good for the remaining clan.

Suddenly a loud horn blared, which was followed by a low rumble. A bright blinding blue light flashed from somewhere close by, but was out of view to Sarain, and when she could see again, she saw that the area was now surrounded with demons. Monsters of all types; claws, fangs, horns, and scales; every kind of unimaginable horror existed in and around their camp. Some beasts pounced on all fours, some flew, and others stood and ran like men.

Sarain's clan members fought as these new intruders bit and clawed them. Men collapsed, torn to shreds, others yelled as they were being eaten alive. Sickening cracks and crunches echoed in her ears as she closed her eyes to shut out the images of blood and gore. Screams rang out from women and children some place in the village, who like her grandfather had said, couldn't out run the demons.

Sarain trembled in her box, but while she was full of fear, something urged her to open her eyes and look on. A few demons did lie dead, but most of the bodies were that of her people. Not many were left standing, but those who were, were all looking at the same thing. She couldn't see what it was, but noticed that the demons had stopped fighting and were now surrounding the group that was left. She saw Orran standing near, he was drenched in blood and sweat, but he was still alive, and Sarain was thankful for that. Her grandfather stood further away, one of his arms looked badly clawed, but he seemed unfazed. A few other men and a couple of women remained, holding weapons, still ready to fight.

Finally the object of her clan's attention came into view. It looked like a man, no, it had to be a vil sang, but the other demons, the full blooded demons, cowered to him in such a way that went against nature. This half demon was massively tall, much more than a man could be, and for a vil sang he looked more like a beast than that of a man. He somewhat resembled a gargoyle statue.

Sarain strained to get a better look, but with legs in the way, was unable to do so. The clan began to rush the colossal creature, striking him with their blades, but they didn't appear to cut. His skin was like stone. The beast lifted his sword and swung it with stride; he sliced a man clean in half. The clan continued to try and chip away at the demon's flesh, but he swatted away their attempts, while grabbing and crushing a man's throat in the process.

Sarain's heart began to race and her stomach grew sick when she saw Orran charge towards the monster. He yelled and thrust his sword at the creature, and hit its arm. Its skin cracked and a trickle of blood seeped out the wound. Orran had injured him, it was just a small scrape, but it gave hope to defeating the beast, because they now knew it could be injured. The creature seemed displeased with Orran, who had become the focus of his interest; he swung his sword at the young man. Orran jumped back, but the tip of the demon's blade grazed him across his chest, cutting into him. It wasn't a fatal wound, but in the moment Sarain saw the blade hit him she without thinking let out a gasp. Orran's eyes and attention immediately went to Sarain's hiding spot, and in that split second, the beast took charge and lunged toward him with incredible speed. He took a hold of the boy and sank his teeth into his neck. It clenched its jaws down, and Orran's sword dropped from his hand. The demon shot his head back up and let Orran's body fall limply to the ground. He landed with a thud, and Sarain had to bite down onto her lip to the point of bleeding just to keep from screaming out. He didn't move; she turned her tear stained face away from the heartbreaking sight.

After a moment she looked up, back to the battle, to see only her grandfather left standing with the beast. Everyone else was dead, and all the other demons remained surrounding him. How did so many fall so fast? She couldn't bear to see the same fate fall upon her grandfather, but there was nothing she could do. She only had basic training in fighting, and wasn't even in the top of her class. How could she possibly save him?

Chapter 9

Sarain opened her eyes to see Kit staring back at her. She must have sensed his eyes in her sleep; she didn't like being stared at.

"Do you always watch people while they're sleeping?" Sarain asked him.

"You were making a lot of noise. It woke me up, and when I came in here you were moving around," Kit told her.

"Oh," Sarain said realizing that she was drenched in sweat. She hadn't been aware that she struggled in her sleep; it wasn't really a surprise though. She sat up in bed. The air was cool against her damp skin. She looked at Kit who looked concerned.

He got up and sat on the edge of the bed then he asked, "Do you always go out hunting?"

"Yes," Sarain simply replied.

"No wonder you have nightmares. Don't you ever do anything for fun?" Kit questioned.

Sarain contemplated for a second and then answered, "No, I can't relax and be happy knowing there's something out there."

"Have you always been like this?" he asked sounding genuinely interested.

The images of violence flashed in Sarain's mind, "I have been for a long time, but no, not always," she spoke trying to remember a better time.

"Hmm," Kit grunted, then after a moment he asked, "whose Orran?"

"What?" Sarain said with surprise.

"You kept calling it out, you sounded really scared," he relayed with worry.

Sarain didn't want to tell Kit the whole truth, so she just responded with, "He was someone I knew a long time ago."

"Is he dead?" Kit curiously asked; not showing any tact for Sarain's feelings, but not trying to be mean either.

She nodded and replied, "Yes, he's dead."

"Sorry," he said quickly.

After a few silent minutes went by, Sarain broke the quiet by asking, "Have you been sleeping okay otherwise?"

"Not really. I used to stay up and wait for Nate to come home, and we would talk about his day when I would try to go to sleep," Kit answered.

"Sounds kind of like a bedtime story," she observed.

"Maybe…" he looked at Sarain for a moment and said, "I've been meaning to ask you. What is up with the purple eyes?"

"Nothing, it's the same reason yours are brown; I was just born that way," she replied.

"It's still weird. Like you have super powers or something," Kit spoke thinking of his comics.

"There's nothing I can do that can't be trained," she said before really thinking over all that she could do. She was a skilled fighter, that was a given; but she wasn't a superhero, was she? Her clan had thought her eye color meant that she would one day be their savior, but it was obvious now that that could never happen. It was most likely a regular abnormality that had occurred in her like people who have albinism or chimeras - people who were two eggs that fused into one, that often give them two different DNA.

Still, Sarain's job did make her stand out, and perhaps she was a bit of a hero, but yet she felt like she could do better, that she wasn't tapping into her full potential. She felt weak and helpless, and hoped that there was more she could do.

She looked to Kit as she got up from bed and said, "Go ahead and lie down, I want to tell you about the time two demons had me trapped in an alley with only a line of barbed wire from a nearby fence to use as a weapon."

It wasn't long before Kit was fast asleep.

Sarain sat in the living room. Hours had gone by, but Kit was still deeply asleep in her bed. She contemplated what she should do about Winston. He was obviously well guarded, possibly by both vil sangs and humans. So it would be best to strike at him during daylight hours when he would be at his weakest. She figured since he ran The Purge, and was usually there until closing, which was just before dawn, then it was likely that it was somewhere there at the club that he slept. She doubted that he slept out in the open, but she hadn't seen in the club where he could be staying. She would have to investigate the club during off hours to see if she could find something she may have missed before. This mission could be a very dangerous one. There appeared to be more vil sang activity there than she was use to. But dangerous or not, she couldn't abandon her job, because the demon activity in this city wouldn't go away until she stopped that club, and she wouldn't let the possibility of death keep her from completing her mission. Only then would she know peace.

A little voice in the back of Sarain's mind reminded her that she now had to take care of Kit. But demon hunting had always come first to her. That wasn't going to change now, and Kit knew that. She also knew that she could never truly be a mother figure to him, and might not be able to fill the void of a sibling either, but she would still be more to him than she had growing up. This was all she could ever do.

Sarain decided that she wasn't going to wait for Kit to wake up; she was going to head down to The Purge while there was still daylight out. She quickly suited up and slipped out the door without as much as a stir from Kit.

From the outside, the club looked empty, but Sarain didn't want to chance an obvious break in through the front door. She climbed the fire escape instead, which led to the roof, but she didn't recall seeing a second floor when she was inside. And she was right; access from the roof to the club had been cut off when the club had at some point been renovated, taking the second floor out to make a vaulted ceiling. She contemplated what she should do next; the front door was the only entrance or exit to the building, which was technically a fire safety hazard, but there was a lot about this club that wasn't up to code. The one entrance was probably so that the occupants inside could keep an easier track on who came and went from the club, and it made a sneak attack nearly impossible.

Sarain looked around the roof top hoping to find anything that could possibly help her and noticed a rather large ventilation duct. The air ducts would have to be large to filter such a sizeable room below, and she did remember seeing ventilation ducts high above the dance floor that twisted their way down to the ground. It wouldn't be an easy trip, and she would have to maneuver her way through some drops, but it would be her best chance of getting in without alerting anyone.

Sarain ripped off the outer screen on the duct, which kept the elements out, and climbed in feet first. If she was going to crawl around in such a tight fitting place, then she was likely to not have room to turn around, and with the drops she would have to make, she rather be dropping feet first than head first. But this meant that she would be crawling backwards through the ventilation.

There was a short drop right away in the duct soon after Sarain had entirely climbed in, but this wasn't a problem. She surprisingly moved quickly and fairly silent through the ventilation. It was dark inside, and Sarain was without a light, but it didn't take long for her eyes to adjust to the dark.

Sarain wasn't sure what she was going to find at the end of all this, perhaps Winston's resting spot, perhaps the resting spot of multiple vil sangs. If there were many, she would have to torch the place down; she couldn't take on more than three at a time. If it were just Winston, she would kill him herself and continue to watch the club for the other vil sangs that frequented it. Now there was a chance that the occupants inside would be awake; vil sangs didn't have to sleep during the day, but usually did since they were nocturnal, and needed their rest just like humans.

Sarain noticed that she was coming upon another drop. This, unlike the first one, would be a considerable drop; a few yards if she remembered right. As she approached it she held herself up and she swung her legs down, crossing them to fit and to use her feet to hold herself up. She crossed her arms as she edged her way down, and used pressure to keep herself from falling. First she would move her hands down, then her feet. She moved slowly, but safely. It took an incredible amount of arm and leg strength to do this, but things like this came naturally to Sarain. After a while, Sarain's feet finally reached the bottom and she uncrossed her legs. She dropped down and backed into the next stretch of air duct, where there was vent that looked down over the club. Sarain maneuvered over it and then peered through it when her head past above it. The club looked empty, dark, and quiet. She was still high up over the dance floor, and wasn't half way through her trip yet. She proceeded to move through many more yards of ventilation and two more drops before finally reaching the bottom.

Sarain managed to turn around to peek through the vent. The coast still looked clear. She gripped onto the vent and pushed it open, still holding on to it so that it wouldn't clatter to the ground. After she climbed out, Sarain went to put the vent back on and realized that she had completely ripped out the bolts that held it on. Funny, she hadn't thought she used that much strength to get the vent off. She set it down, and proceeded to look around the club. Near the entrance where the restrooms were located there was a third door. It was locked, but not so complicated that Sarain couldn't get it open with some simple lock picking techniques.

Inside the room was a regular looking office. There was a desk, a filing cabinet, and a bookcase. Sarain scanned over the title of books. Some were random encyclopedia letters, not a complete set, a few collections of short stories and poems, even a couple of fancy looking cook books; but all were dusty and seemed to only be there for appearances. Scanning around the room, everything looked to be in place, in fact things looked too in place; the office didn't look like it had been used in some time. The desk was clean of debris and only had a few pens and unimportant papers inside it. The filing cabinet contained business documents, and nothing out of the ordinary.

Sarain sighed; this was looking like a wasted trip. She couldn't find one real peculiar thing, nor could she find any evidence of a resting place for Winston. She lowered her head while brushing her hand through her hair in stress. Something caught her eye. It was a piece of paper under one of the legs of the desk, it was brightly colored and probably just a club flyer, but the fact that it was there was odd enough, since the rest of the office was so pristine from clutter. Sarain pushed on the desk to slide it off the paper. She didn't want to tear it trying to get it up, but the desk didn't budge. She gave the desk a once over with a confused look, as it didn't appear heavy. She pushed again, but still it didn't move. Finally she stopped and examined the desk. It looked normal, but she inspected the left side more closely, the side with the drawers. She had to crouch down to get a good look at its legs, and realized that the desk's two left legs were bolted down to the floor. She gave a closer look to the floor; it was plain checkered linoleum tile, but the grooves around the edging of the tile under the desk didn't look as tightly spaced.

Sarain grabbed a hold of the right side of the desk and lifted it up, and with it came a section of the floor. It was a hidden trap door. The desk's weight sat perfectly on its side leaving the door able to be left propped open. She peered inside; there were steps, but she couldn't see much more, it was too dark. She wasn't sure how far or deep the place went, but this was what she had been looking for, and she couldn't back out now.

She pulled out a lighter, she hadn't used it earlier in the vent, because she didn't have room or the capability to use it and crawl at the same time. She put her foot on the first step; it was solid, and proceeded to walk down secret corridor.

While she took her steps into darkness, the thought occurred to Sarain that there was a chance she would never see daylight again.

Chapter 10

The steps led to a dimly lit hallway. Sarain put her lighter away. Wall sconces holding small candles lined the hallway, giving off just enough light to see where she was going. Sarain wondered if this was more for decoration; she had thought vil sangs could see well in the dark. But since they were only half demons, perhaps their night vision was only a little keener than humans. At the end of the hallway was a door, it looked heavy and was closed. There was no lock on it, just a handle. She pulled the door open, and it groaned. She quickly stopped the door from going any further and hoped that its noise had not been heard. The passageway was quiet. Sarain squeezed through the little opening that she had made, and slowly let the heavy door close.

On the other side of the door was a spiraling stone staircase. It had no railing, but one side was always against the wall. Sconces still lit the way, and as Sarain leaned over the edge of the spiraling stairs, she could see candles lighting a long way down.

Sarain wondered how many candles were in this passage, and how often they needed to be changed out.

Lighting and replacing them couldn't be a fun job. Did the vil sangs go to a store regularly for that kind of thing? Electricity would be more practical, but how would you explain such a corridor to an electrician? Either way, the place still seemed to be a tad bit overdramatic to Sarain, she couldn't understand why these creatures always went with the stereotypes.

The deeper she went down the staircase, the thinner and muskier the air got; perhaps it was the depth or perhaps it was all the little flames burning away at the oxygen, but Sarain felt herself getting lightheaded. Maybe that was why there were so many candles and why this place was going so deep; to keep air-breathing humans out. She steadied herself against the wall, and waited a moment to catch her breath. She had come too far to turn back.

Sarain regained her balance and continued on. She finally arrived at the bottom, and noticed that the passage broke off into two different directions. One led to a door, and the other led to another long hallway. She was a little sick of long stretches so she opted for the door. She opened this door more softly and slowly than the previous; it didn't even so much as creak.

Sarain glanced inside; it was another hallway, this one with many doors lined up on one side. Perhaps they were bedrooms, or more passageways, but she felt as though she shouldn't investigate this area quite yet. Instead, she turned back, and headed in the opposite direction to the other hallway near the stairs. It stretched out far and had one door at the end of it. Sarain wondered how greatly these passageways wound; it felt like a labyrinth.

She reached the new door, and listened for any sounds. Silence. She opened it and saw another long hallway with a door at the end, but about halfway down the hallway there was a turn; where it led she couldn't see, but it was still having less options and possibilities than the last hallway, which she liked, since it gave less of a chance of her getting lost.

Sarain started to walk through the door when a thought popped into her head: How much time had gone by since she had first arrived at the club; Two hours, three, or even more? Was it night already? She cursed herself for not having a watch; they beeped, glowed, and light could shine off them, all making them a risk for her, but now underground it would come in handy.

Sarain's nerves began to get the better of her and she started to back out the new door when she suddenly heard a thud behind her. It was night time. She quickly spun around and saw a thin man standing in the doorway to the hall with many doors that she had just been at only a few minutes earlier. He looked human enough, but was rather pale; Sarain knew better. He looked at her confused for a moment, as though he were trying to recollect who she was.

Sarain wasn't going to wait for him to make a move, so she dashed towards the stairs, and the man ran after her. She moved quickly, but the stairs were regrettably closer to the vil sang. The glow in his eyes flared up and Sarain could see his fangs. Its okay, the voice in her head said, it's only one, you can handle one. She whipped out her machete, but soon more vil sangs piled out from the same door like some silent alarm had gone off; two more, four more, ten.

The first vil sang yelled out, "Intruder!" then shortly added, "She was heading towards the master's chambers!"

Sarain lunged for the steps, feeling her feet fly off the ground. With amazement she jumped over the heads of the vil sangs and crash landed on the stairs. The stone steps did not make for a soft landing, pain shot threw her body, but she held on tight to her blade.

The vil sangs rushed after her. Sarain scrambled to get on her feet, but one of the larger men grabbed her by her leg and dragged her down. Her head thumped against a step and cut open. Blood trickled down the side of her face. Another vil sang flipped her over, and she caught a glimpse of a familiar face. Winston stood watching from behind a few men, his eyes were wide as he recognized the intruder. He didn't make an attempt to attack her, he just watched as the other men proceeded to grab and kick at her.

Sarain let out a yell, kicking at the beasts. One held down her arm trying to take her machete away, but she broke free from its grasp, and sliced off its hand. The vil sang roared in pain and backed off, but the others proceeded to swarm. Another grabbed her other arm and bit down. She screamed in pain, but this bold move proved fatal for the brave beast as it left him in the perfect position for Sarain to chop off his head.

The headless demon's body collapsed buying Sarain some time to get on her feet. She started up the steps, but stumbled when a sudden sharp pain hit her side. Time seemed to slow down as she heard the thumping of her own heartbeat. Sarain looked down at her side and saw the handle of a blade sticking out just beneath her rib cage. Apparently one of the vil sangs had been armed; she hadn't noticed. Her free hand went to the knife and she felt herself pulling it out. A spray of blood left with the blade, but instead of dropping the weapon, she quickly turned around, sending more pain shooting to the wound.

Sarain could see Winston still standing aback, just watching everything unfold. He was the source of her problems, he may not be doing the fighting, but she was here because of him. Her hate for him raged inside of her, her arm went back and she flung the knife at him. It hit the wall a few inches away from Winston's head; the shock of it sent a stunned look on his face. The blade was stuck half way in, it had hit with much force. Next time Sarain swore she wouldn't miss.

She hurried up the stairs, the vil sangs not far behind her. She limped, clutching her side, but the adrenaline kept her moving swiftly. It was surprising to even her how she managed to out run these creatures; these non-men specialized in heightened abilities; faster speeds, more strength, and yet while being out numbered, Sarain was able to escape still breathing.

The trip up the spiral staircase seemed shorter than the trip down it. Sarain burst through the hallway door and up the steps leading to the office. She hastily grabbed the raised desk and sent it slamming down; smearing her bloody hand print along the top. She came bursting out the office and saw the large guard standing at the club entrance, having just opened the door. The look on his face was of pure astonishment. He reached for Sarain as she approached, but she lifted her hands up in the air, and one look at the machete that she clung to sent the guard diving out of the way.

Sarain was out the door and down the street in a matter of seconds. A gust of cool night air hit her like a wave of relief. Her hand went back to her side which was now soaked in blood. She couldn't go to the hospital; they would ask too many questions and it just plain wasn't safe enough. A vil sang could easily walk into a hospital, and that would be where they would expect her to go anyway. She had to go home; she was losing too much blood, and couldn't wait till dawn.

Sarain gave a quick glimpse behind her, she wasn't being followed. She went a few miles, still running in a hurry, before she finally began to slow down to a stagger.

By the time she reached her domicile, she was dragging. The view of it at that instant was the first time it felt like a home. She burst through her door giving Kit a fright, with blood dripping down her leg. She screamed for him to get her the first aid kit, which was located in the bathroom. He hesitated from panic for a moment, and

Sarain screamed at him again. Finally he rushed off to retrieve it, and came back quickly clinging it to his chest.

Sarain had him set the first aid kit on the table, then opened it up and rifled through it. She pulled out gauze, tape, antiseptic, and a needle and thread. She pulled off her bloody shirt and poured the antiseptic on her side. She let out a scream that caused Kit to jump back. Her attention then turned to him and she said, "Kit, I need you to do me a favor."

His eyes looked scared as he stared at her while she said, "I need you to hold my side closed while I sew it shut."

Kit didn't have much choice, he did as told, and Sarain's screams could be heard from down the street. The same street where a lone figure stood watching upon the small home; a figure whose eyes glowed a vibrant blue from the recognition of the scent of Sarain's blood.

Chapter 11

Sarain lay limp and exhausted in bed. Kit had fallen asleep next to her; like a child worried over his mother, he stayed by her side all night, afraid that his new guardian might slip away from him. She had slept, but still needed much more rest to recuperate for the events of the night before. Her side still throbbed and had become bruised. The gash on her head had sealed and was healing nicely. Sarain in all was sore, but she was alive, and grateful for it.

Her actions from that night kept playing out in her head, she knew what she had done wrong, but she couldn't figure out how she managed to escape. She had pushed herself harder than she had ever done before, and such actions like jumping over the vil sangs, and running so quickly after such a bad stab wound were things than she had never done before. Sarain felt like she was growing stronger.

She got up from the bed with a groan. Kit opened his eyes and looked up. He quickly sat up in bed and asked, "Do you need my help?"

Sarain groaned again and said, "No, I'm alright, sore, but alright."

Kit watched as Sarain moved around and asked, "Should you really be up and walking around like that? Won't you rip your stitches or something?"

"It's okay," she told him, "I heal fast."

Kit gave her a frumpy look like he didn't believe her, but it was true; she did heal fast, she always had. He got up and made Sarain breakfast for a change. This was something she could get used to. It was just simple scrambled eggs, but she appreciated the gesture.

Kit sat down at the table, across from Sarain and asked, "Are you going out again tonight?"

"No, not tonight," she rapidly replied, "I'm still too sore to fight."

"Good," the boy responded in a tone like he wouldn't let Sarain leave anyway.

She smiled at Kit realizing his concern for her; she wasn't used to someone worrying about her. She found it rather endearing, but her thoughts soon turned troubled; she had lost all chance of catching Winston with his guard down. After last night he and his men would be on full alert. While she did manage to kill one vil sang and wounded another, who knew how many more were down in those catacombs under The Purge. It was obviously the city's haven for the demon kind. It was a lot bigger of a job than she was used to dealing with.

She would have to give it time before making another move, if she didn't scrap the mission altogether.

She had never abandoned a job before, but she had Kit to look out for now, and the vil sangs would be out looking for her at this point; she had made herself known. Perhaps this one was just too much for her.

Sarain sat outside breathing in the cool air; this was the first night in a long time that she hadn't gone hunting. She had forgotten how nice it could be to just stop and look up at the stars. Maybe she could go straight for a while, for Kit's sake. Get set up in a new place, and get a real job. Sarain knew that these were just empty dreams; she would find herself walking the streets again, hunting for creatures that lurked in the shadows. This is what she did, this is all she knew.

Sarain sat alone; Kit was inside, probably reading a comic. She had needed time to herself to think, so she had come outside, promising Kit that she wouldn't leave the curb. She thought of her mother, whom she had very few memories of. Her mother had died of an illness when Sarain was only five, but she remembered her mother being special; extraordinarily special to her clan.

Sarain wondered how much different her life would have been if her mother would have lived, or her clan. Would her life still be so filled with demons? Her clan of people who trained and taught the ways how to destroy the beasts; a clan of warriors who for centuries hunted the creatures, but even with that, her life hadn't seemed so surrounded by demons until that fateful night.

Was it really her choice to abandon the path that had been so strongly forced upon her? She felt that no matter where she hid or ran off to, that her mission would still find her. But she was tired, so very tired.

Sarain sat there thinking. She heard the sounds of footsteps coming up behind her, and she said to Kit, "So you finally came out to get me."

"I didn't realize that you were expecting me," a deep voice replied.

Sarain's eyes went wide, that wasn't Kit's voice. She immediately spun around and saw Winston standing behind her. Her hand went to her side before she recalled that she hadn't brought a weapon out with her.

Winston noted the look of surprise on her face and said, "Perhaps it wasn't me you were expecting."

Sarain jumped up and backed away from him, then looked to her house, and thought of Kit. No, with the barrier around it Winston wouldn't be able to get inside.

Winston took a small step closer to Sarain and stated, "You're not really one for words, are you?"

"It's foolish for you to come here," she said, ignoring his comment.

"Foolish? I don't see why, you're wounded and appear to be unarmed. Foolish is walking into a den of demons alone," he said making an observation.

"You're just a weak half breed. The vil sang name alone means vile blood; even the dirt thinks you're filthy," she declared to him.

Winston "tsked" her and took another step closer while saying, "Those are strong words from someone who can barely stand," then he gave her a once over and said, "Then again, maybe you weren't as seriously injured as I thought," he stopped short from approaching and asked, "Didn't you hit you head last night?"

Sarain felt her forehead, the scar was already gone. So she replied, "That was barely even a scratch."

"A scratch that gushed blood?" Winston questioned. He looked at her curiously.

Just then the door to the house came bursting open, and Kit came running out yelling, "Sarain!" Evidently he had noticed that his injured guardian had company.

Winston peered over his shoulder at the boy, and Sarain quickly shouted with panic, "Kit, get back inside!"

Kit stood there for a moment, looking worried, he didn't want to leave Sarain alone, but did as told and hurried back inside.

Winston turned back around, apparently uninterested in the boy and said, "Sarain, so that's your name. I really don't know why you couldn't just tell me yourself."

"What is your obsession with knowing my name? Does it really matter who it is that is going to kill you?" Sarain pressed on.

"You do like to talk big, don't you? I think you are the one who is obsessing over me; showing up at my work, my home, interrupting my private moments. I never did anything to you. And now you've gone and made a lot of people angry. This is not a game little girl, and you apparently don't stand well against many, so why do you keep trying to get yourself killed?" Winston proclaimed, wanting to get his point across.

"Why are you even here? If you're going to kill me then do it already, I'm tired of listening to your rambling," Sarain stated with exhaustion. She was tired, tired of fighting an endless supply of monsters, and now having to deal with them mocking her on her own ground. If Winston wanted to kill her, she would let him, she wasn't going to fight back, not tonight.

Winston stared at her as though searching through his thoughts. Sarain didn't bother to wonder what he was thinking, she didn't care; she just wanted this to end.

He finally broke the silence by saying, "I prefer my fights to be fair. Even though I may be 'filth' as you so poignantly point out, I still have my standards."

"Fine, then leave," Sarain gruffly said, then she made a bold move, she walked right past Winston, leaving her back to him. It left her open to an easy attack, but this didn't make a difference to her, either way. He stayed standing as she past him by, making no attempt to attack her, true to his word. Sarain walked to her house, opened the door, and went inside without giving him a further look.

Winston waited for a while, half expecting for Sarain to come back with a weapon, but she didn't. He looked back at her house. The night was still early, but his rendezvous with her was over, for now.

He started to walk off, down the street. A few yards away a creature stirred in the shadows of an alleyway, having watched the whole scene play out from its unseen hiding spot. It stepped out, approaching Winston.

It was a short creature, but its sharp scales and long claws made it a formidable monster. It stared up at him with large red eyes, and spoke in a high raspy voice, "Why didn't you kill the girl?"

"Not yet, it would have been too easy," Winston said not looking his hideous companion in the eye.

"Easy is all the better, but the difficulty should make no difference, you should do as you are told. The master will not like this," it said to him with alarm in its tone.

"Let me worry about him, you are not his second in command," Winston stated forcefully to the small beast.

The creature backed off with a shuffle, but stared him down. Winston ignored its empty attempt of a threat, and left the little demon standing alone. It gave Sarain's house one last look through the corner of its eye, and then followed Winston into the night.

Chapter 12

Sarain darted back and forth through the rooms of her domicile. She grabbed what few things she had and shoved them into the two duffle bags on her bed. Kit had already packed up the bag that he had brought with him when he came to live with Sarain. He now sat there on the floor against the wall, trying to keep out of the way; his eyes followed her as she moved about so franticly.

Sarain was in a panic, the enemy knew where she lived; it was a mistake she had never made before. She had hidden her distress well enough from Winston the night before, but she wasn't going to wait for him to come back.

Sarain had already purchased bus tickets for her and Kit, and they would be leaving town the next day; the soonest she could get. It would bring them to a new city for a new start, and it would be hard at first for Sarain to get established, especially having to care for a child now, but she would do her all to make sure that Kit was safe and provided for. But this wasn't her worry now, protecting him was.

In the meantime, Sarain had put a fresh barrier around the house, so that she would have peace of mind. While the beasts did know where she lived, it was still safer than a motel; a motel, with so many people coming and going, couldn't be properly sealed, nor would she have enough herbs and supplies to try.

Sarain figured that it would be a few days before Winston would come back looking for her, if he indeed wanted a fair fight. She knew that he had an inkling that she healed fast, but he couldn't possibly know exactly how fast. She felt her side, where her stab wound had once been, now it looked like a mere scratch. Kit was curious as well to how Sarain had healed so fast, but she wasn't sure if she could properly explain it to him, nor was she sure that he would believe her.

Sarain stopped and glanced around. That was everything, except for a shoebox in the back of her closet; something that she kept in case she would ever need it. She called it her emergency kit. Inside it was a red dress, sunglasses, perfume, and a blond wig; simple things that Sarain did not like to use. She knew that one day she might need a disguise if her presence had ever become compromised. The wig was obviously to alter her appearance; it was made with human hair and was in a common style so that she wouldn't stand out. The sunglasses were to hide her eyes, something that could easily give her away. The red dress, while it was an attracting color, women frequently wore it at night, when the creatures hunting for her would be out. It was such an extreme change from her normal attire, that someone looking for her wouldn't expect her to wear it. And lastly the perfume was high in oils and would cover her scent and last for a good while after being sprayed.

Sarain stared down at the contents of the box, she knew what she wanted to do with the disguise, but Kit would never agree to it, and he deserved a say in this too. Nevertheless there was something that still bothered her about the day she went down into the catacombs under The Purge. One of the vil sangs had commented that she had been heading towards the master's chambers, which would have been down the hall further from the stairs, and then down another long hall after that. But yet, soon after she was attacked, Winston was already standing in the background, leaving her to believe that he had to have come from the same door as the other vil sangs. So then, would that mean that he wasn't their master, even though he ran The Purge?

If there was a greater beast down there, one that for some reason couldn't let itself be seen by the public, then Sarain wanted to know why. She had found plenty of hideous demons wandering out on the streets at night, and while they did try to stay hidden, they wouldn't spend all their time underground. Besides, this demon had to be fearsome enough to get other creatures to do its bidding.

Sarain closed her eyes; she knew she couldn't just walk away, not without one final attempt. There would only be another night before their bus would leave, and that last night would be tonight.

Sarain slipped into the revealing red dress. She strapped her machete to her thigh - the only place she could hide it - and attached her switchblade to her shoe. They weren't the most elegant footwear, but she doubted anyone would be looking at her feet. She adjusted the wig, it wasn't really her color, but with her pale skin it didn't really matter. She sprayed the perfume over her body, it was a strong scent, but it was not her scent, and that was what she needed.

Sarain stepped out into the living room, and Kit looked up at her with his eyes wide. "Where are you going dressed like that?" he asked with astonishment.

Sarain gave him a look to let him know not to pry, but Kit got up and said loudly, "No, you are not going after that man!" After a moment of Sarain still not explaining herself, Kit added, "You got hurt so bad last time, can't you just stay here?"

Sarain gazed down at Kit and said, "If my actions tonight could stop what happened to your brother from happening to someone else, wouldn't you want me to do it?"

Kit gave her a pout. Sarain knew that she hadn't given him a fair choice, but there was a bigger picture to look at, and her strength had to be shared and put to use. He finally nodded with a sad face and Sarain gave him a smile. She looked down and saw that he was wearing her ankh necklace.

"I'm glad that you're still wearing that," she said gesturing to the ankh, she then changed to another subject by saying, "I'm going to need you to keep all the lights off while I'm gone and to not make a sound. It's better if it looks like no one is home. And I'm sure I don't need to tell you to not leave the house."

Sarain began to head for the door, but stopped short and said, "If I don't make it back in time, I want you to get on that bus without me, and not to worry."

Kit's eyes turned sad and he asked, "But you will come, right?"

Sarain looked up at him and replied, "Sure I will."

They both knew it was a lie, but neither said anything else about it. Kit gave Sarain a hug goodbye, and tried to play it off as a hug for good luck, but he held on a bit too long, and she heard him sniffle when his face was behind her back.

Sarain closed the door behind her as she stepped out and waited, leaning against it until the lights turned off before she left. She put on her sunglasses and headed down the street towards the club.

She thought of Kit as she walked, she hoped she wouldn't be leaving him forever like his family had done before her. He was a strong child, but growing up alone was easy for no one.

Chapter 13

The club was crowded again tonight with many people still waiting to get in. Sarain waited in line with everyone else and even struck up a conversation with a woman standing nearby hoping that she would blend in. The woman was a college student who was there with friends, and had obviously had a few drinks before coming there. She was rather cheerful and embracing to the attention of a stranger, and complimented Sarain on her great wardrobe. The large guard was at the door again, and Sarain couldn't let herself be recognized. When she approached the door she addressed her new acquaintance again, who threw an arm around her making it look like they were there together. The large guard ushered them in unaware of Sarain's true identity.

Shortly after entering, she parted ways with her new friend, who was making her way to the bar, and Sarain made her own way to the restrooms. The office door was closed, but Sarain turned into the ladies room, and after a minute inside she peeked out, and made sure the coast was clear. No one appeared to be looking, so Sarain slipped out and backed up towards the office door. She tried the knob, and sure enough, the door was unlocked. She expected as much since it was night, and the vil sangs would be coming and going. She quickly stepped inside and noticed that the previous desk had been replaced with a bigger, heavier looking one. She didn't know if this was to keep people out of the lair below or if it was because her blood had stained the last one, but she knew that this new desk would not keep her out.

The new desk was indeed heavier, being made out of some kind of stone. It probably would take two or three human men to move it, but wouldn't be a challenge for a vil sang. Sarain wasn't sure if she could lift it, she had never bench pressed weights, and wasn't sure what her limit would be. She went to the right side of the desk to get a grip on the desk's end when the office door suddenly came flying open.

A man dressed like one of the bartenders stood in the doorway looking at Sarain for a moment before he finally asked, "What are you doing in here? This is for employees only."

Sarain leaned over the desk flirtatiously and said, "I was looking for your cute boss."

The man stepped in and closed the door behind him, he approached Sarain saying, "The boss is busy, but I'm free for a little fun, baby."

Sarain smiled at him, feeling awkward; she wasn't used to come-ons, but she was especially not used to acting loose. The man walked over to her and gave her a closer once over. Sarain smiled at him again and asked, "Do you like what you see?"

The man smiled back, and started to put his arm around her while responding, "Oh yes."

"Good," Sarain said softly to him, then she grabbed his arm and pulled it down while sweep kicking his feet out from under him. He knocked his head against the desk and was out cold. Sarain looked him over; he was human, probably just a regular club employee. She dragged him over and laid him against the wall next to the bookcase. Upon a quick inspection he wouldn't be noticed, unless someone really stepped in and looked around the office.

Sarain went back to the desk. She grabbed the end of it and crouched down, bending at the knees. She groaned as she lifted the heavy desk, but was surprised that she managed to lift it up. She couldn't leave it lying on its side this time, not with so many people nearby and able to peek in the office. And locking the door would alert anyone who knew that it should be open. Instead she had to hold the desk up as she stepped into the tunnel, and slowly lowered it shut with each step down. This would make a quick escape difficult if Sarain had need for it again, but it was a chance she had to take.

Candles still lit the hallway, but Sarain proceeded with caution. She removed her sunglasses so it would be easier for her to see; in this instance hiding her eyes would be pointless. She didn't know if the vil sangs had left any new traps for her, nor did she know if she could be expecting any of them to walk in or out suddenly. She figured coming at night would be something they wouldn't anticipate her doing, being such a bold move. But really, her chances were good that there were now less vil sangs in the tunnels below, since they could be out looking for prey at this hour. Given the ones that were below would be awake, but Sarain could handle vil sangs in smaller numbers quite easily.

Sarain made it to the first door without incident. She opened it slowly, remembering that it groaned the last time, and stopped it short before opening it all the way. She squeezed through and then advanced to the spiraling staircase. The last time she was on these steps she had been mobbed and badly injured. She looked over the side and the steps still looked a long way down, she would have to proceed more quietly this time since ears would be alert and awake. Sarain took off her shoes and carried them down with her. Her bare feet on the stone steps made no sound whatsoever, but the stairs were cold so deep beneath the ground. She trotted down the steps quickly, not having to worry about making noise, but she made sure to listen for any possible sound of movement beneath her. All was silent.

It didn't feel like it took Sarain as long to reach the bottom of the stairs as it had the first time. As she took the final steps down she saw a blood stain on one of the stairs; her blood stain, where she had cracked open her head when being dragged down. Sarain then glanced at the wall and saw a spray mark from when she pulled out the knife that had been stuck in her side. That had only been a couple nights before, and now Sarain walked fine as if she had never been injured, but these stains told how she almost died.

She put on her shoes, preparing to walk on, and then heard a rustling sound coming from the hallway behind the door that so many vil sangs came piling out before. Sarain unlaced the strap holding on her machete to her thigh, and grasped it tightly in her hand. She pressed her back against the stairwell wall and waited for whatever made the noise to appear. The sound of the door swinging open echoed in the hall. Sarain held her breath so not to make a sound. Footsteps headed towards the stairway, and soon a pale man turned the corner.

He noticed Sarain's red dress first, and then he noticed her eyes. A startled expression came over his a face just before his head rolled off his body. Sarain had sliced off his head without hesitation. The vil sang's body slumped to the ground, and blood spurted out from the gaping hole in its neck. It was a good thing Sarain was wearing red.

She looked down at the remains, and observed that the beast had only had one hand. He was the same vil sang the she had injured previously; he wouldn't be attacking her anymore.

Sarain stepped over the body, and headed for the hallway furthest from the stairs. She would have to move quicker now, before another vil sang came along and saw the body, and alerted the others.

Down the hall was a door, Sarain remembered this, and behind the door was another long hall and another door, as well as a turn that left its destination unseen. She headed straight, possibly to the "Master's chambers". When she neared the turn in the hallway, she slowed down and peered around the corner. It was another lengthy hallway that led to another door, it was a sight that Sarain had already seen much of down there, but for some reason the look of it made her stomach quiver. Something laid behind that door that brought fear to her bones. Perhaps it was just her nerves, but Sarain did not want to find out what waited in that direction. She continued straight to the nearest door. As she approached it she stepped softly listening for possible sounds on the other side.

Sarain pressed her ear against the door, but could hear nothing. She gently pushed it open, and slipped inside.

The new room was sizeable, and looked to be a small arena. There were stone columns giving up support, and pews carved into the rock ground, to fit many onlookers. The room could hold several beasts. The rows of seats were like bleachers in a stadium, descending lower with each row until finally ending at a leveled ground where a podium stood.

Down on the leveled ground was where Sarain saw two figures standing. One was a small demon with long claws and scaly skin; it had big red eyes that even Sarain could see from this distance. The other appeared to be an extremely tall demon, not just tall compared to the dwarf sized creature next to it, but much taller than what a mortal man could be. This beast's back was turned to Sarain leaving her unable to get a better look. But she could see that he had pointed ears, gray skin, and claw-like hands. He stood upright unlike most demons, and his body shape, while big, was more like a man. And he wore a robe, when demons usually preferred to walk nude.

Sarain strained to hear what was being said from behind one of the stone pillars. The little demon was explaining something to the taller beast, the creature sounded scared like he was worried about disappointing his superior.

He spoke in a high raspy voice and said, "Master, we are bringing in as many people as we can, but there are fewer out on the streets these days. The criminals and delinquents were much easier, because the police weren't looking for them, but a lot of these new people are bringing up questions."

Sarain had recalled hearing that a lot of people had been going missing lately, but since the crime level was so low, she hadn't put much thought in it. But if they were taking the criminals, then it was a no wonder why these people weren't being missed. She thought of Nate, who wasn't a bad kid, but aside from Kit, he didn't have any real personal ties to grieve for him. They were taking the city's outcasts, most likely through the club, and doing god knows what with them. They had turned Nate, so perhaps they were turning the others, but where were they if they were still missing?

They were here, under the club, somewhere in this labyrinth of tunnels. But why so many?

Sarain's thoughts were broken when she heard the deep booming voice of the bigger beast begin to talk, "I don't care if there are questions, I need more, my army is not yet complete!"

Army! The images of Sarain's massacred clan flashed into her mind. Another army was being made, that meant more people were going to die. Would it be another raid on another clan somewhere, or just a full out chaotic attack?

No, Sarain couldn't let that happen again. She edged her way down the steps, staying hidden, but moving closer to this master demon; if she was ever going to have a chance to take him out, then now was it. With only him and one other small beast, this would be her best chance at a fair fight.

Sarain took a few more steps closer then halted when she heard the master demon ask, "And how is the progress going with the intruder?"

"She will no longer be a problem; it is being taken care of at this moment," the small demon said in its high voice.

Sarain stopped breathing and felt her heart sink to the pit of her stomach. She was the intruder, but she was there in the catacombs, safely hidden. That meant they thought she was home…with Kit.

Sarain took a deep breath realizing that if she had any chance of saving him she would have to move quickly and leave now. The master demon would have to wait.

Chapter 14

Sarain raced up the spiral staircase. Her dress ripped up the leg in the process; she ran in long strides jumping from step to step causing the fabric of her dress to stretch until the point of tearing. It felt like she couldn't run fast enough no matter how hard she pushed herself. But Sarain was back under the office before she knew it, she grabbed a hold of the trap door that was weighted down by a heavy desk on top and threw it open without trouble.

In the room above she noticed that the employee she had left unconscious was gone; she didn't care, but figured that he would most likely have assumed that she had just taken off, since an alarm was never called. Odds were that no one would even know she had been there until they found the body of the vil sang she killed waiting down in the tunnels below.

Sarain ran out of the office, never bothering to fix the desk. She pushed past people on the way to the exit, knocking a few completely over. She didn't care who she hurt, she just needed them out of the way. A couple of club goers shouted profanities at her in protest, but little else was done. The large guard took notice of her rampage, and tried to stop her on the way out. He grabbed her by the waist while saying, "Slow down." But Sarain simply elbowed him in the gut, causing him to wretch forward and let her go. She didn't think he ever actually recognized her.

She sped down the club stairs and out into the street. The night air was cold, but Sarain could only feel the heat of rage growing inside her. How could she have left Kit alone? Why had she stupidly believed that Winston wanted a fair fight? Of course he wouldn't fight fair; he had demon blood coursing through his veins. But why play these games? No, it didn't matter, this was her fault; she took Kit in, and then she failed to watch out for him.

As Sarain's anger grew, her legs began to move faster; they felt like they were on fire while her surroundings started to blur. Cars went weaving by, some blaring their horns, but she didn't have concern to move out of the street. Miles of road rapidly went by in a flash, and soon Sarain was drawing up on her house, or what remained of it.

Her home lay in rubble; charred pieces of wood and cinder sat where her house once stood. She knew this meant that once the demons realized they couldn't get in due to the barrier that they instead burnt her house down, hoping to make its occupants come running out.

But what of Kit? Had he stayed in the burning building or did he run out to be captured by the demons?

Sarain wasn't sure which of these gruesome fates she preferred, but she had no hope of finding Kit alive.

She climbed into the wreckage and searched through the still hot and smoking debris with a temperature so high that it began to melt the rubber on her shoes. She stepped through where her living room had once been, where she had spent meals with Kit and had watched him sleep. Part of a wall that used to divide into her bedroom still remained, but the bed and her belongings were gone, all turned into ash.

Sarain glanced around and saw no sign of Kit. She prayed for once that he had disobeyed her and left the house before the beasts had ever come, but she knew that this was just a desperate dream. Nevertheless she had to try; "Kit!" she yelled out, hoping for an answer. Silence. "KIT!" she screamed again, but still nothing. She would have given anything to hear the boy's voice at that moment.

Sarain could feel the tears welling up in her eyes; she had lost the closest thing she had had to family in a long time, and it was her own misjudgment that had led to this misfortune. Grief started to overcome her, so much so that she almost didn't hear the footsteps sneaking up behind her. A sudden snap of wood caused Sarain to go shooting up, her machete in hand, and she spun around to face the prowler.

A group mixed with both vil sangs and full blooded demons stood before her. They had evidently been waiting for her to return, but Kit was definitely not with them, they must have already disposed of him. Sarain found it funny that they would work together; demons normally looked down on vil sangs, but she figured that they must have made an exception for her. There were fifteen total, more than she had ever faced at one time. The vil sangs would be easier to pick off. She could in no way manage to pull off killing the whole group, but if this was going to be her end, then she would take as many with her as she could.

The beasts rushed her within seconds. Sarain dodged the first couple of lunges, and sliced the head off of a slower moving vil sang. A slimy looking demon dove at her feet, and Sarain jumped up over him then came crashing down on top of him, thrusting her blade into his back and all the way out through his chest; she was fairly sure that she got through to its heart.

Next, a vil sang charged her, but he did so in a sloppy manner, leaving himself open for Sarain to drive her blade into his gut and rip it upward, slicing him mostly in half. Shortly thereafter, two demons lunged toward her, one on either side. Sarain was able to slice one across the chest, but the other successfully tackled her to the ground. It dug its claws into her back, and she could feel it ripping away at her flesh.

The other creatures took this cue to horde in; eyes glowing and fangs exposed, they swatted and clawed at her. The vil sangs mostly punched and kicked, a few egged the others on. Sarain took the beating without even so much as a scream; this seemed to disappoint a few. The thrashing went on for a few minutes until finally one of the demons stopped to say, "Enough!" It spoke in a deep hoarse voice, and said, "You know the drill, the master wants her alive."

Alive? Was killing her not enough? No, Sarain thought to herself, this must mean they plan to… Sarain choked up blood as she struggled to cry out, "Just kill me!"

One of the vil sangs, who now looked like just another pale man, gazed down at her in disgust. He brought back his fist, and the last thing she heard was, "Shut up, meat!"

Everything went black after that.

Sarain's vision was blurry when she came through. She felt dizzy, like the walls were moving, and then she grasped that she was being dragged. It was dark, but after a moment, she recognized where she was; in the tunnels under The Purge. She felt limp and broken, too weak to fight the beasts that were moving her. She was in the hall heading towards the master's chambers, but then she realized that they were turning. They were taking her in the direction of the door that had given her chills earlier, and she was going to find out what lied behind it that sent waves so strongly to her that it called out to a sixth sense.

Sarain began to struggle, using what little energy she had. One of the creatures carrying her looked down at her and said to the other demon, "It looks like the girl is awake, let's hurry before she causes us more trouble."

They quickened pace, and Sarain began to scream. She thrashed hoping to break free, but only made a ruckus. The door creaked opened and she was pulled inside.

Chapter 15

The room was dark and damp. Rows of bricked cells were on either side. Mold grew on the walls and only a few candles lit the musky room. The beasts dragged Sarain into a den at the end of a hall, and there, there was an old oak torture chair. The creatures dropped the beaten Sarain into the chair, and one held her still as the other clamped her arms in.

Sarain knew she needed to fight, but could barely lift her head - she had lost a lot of blood. Still she managed to muster up and say, "What are you doing with me?"

"We need to make sure you won't fight when the master comes in," one of the demons said, surprisingly insightful. Sarain had expected to be ignored.

They finished clamping her in, and then immediately positioned themselves to the back of the room, behind her. Sarain waited, propped up in the chair. The den was better lit than anywhere else in this little torture chamber. It was also damp, and smelled of urine; Sarain was pretty sure it was from previous occupants of the chair. She looked up and her eyes focused on something she found strange to be in these mucky catacombs - it was a television screen. She wasn't sure how it was powered but it looked clean and new.

This is not promising, Sarain thought to herself. She heard a door opened behind her, and the sounds of thumping made by heavy feet followed.

"Leave us," a deep voice said from behind her, which was followed by retreating footsteps and a door closing.

The heavy footsteps began again, and Sarain could see a large shadow approaching on the wall. After a moment the huge gray demon stepped around and in front of her. The master - finally Sarain was able to get a good look at his face, though things were still somewhat blurry. His pointed ears looked lengthy from front view, his jaws were elongated, his brow bone protruded, and his eyes were and glowed a constant yellow, but aside from all these hideous disfigurations, the rest of his facial features were completely human. Sarain realized that he wasn't an actual demon, he was a vil sang, or at least one that had to have been made directly from a full blooded demon, causing the virus to be stronger and run more rapidly through his veins; this was the result of what demon blood could do with you after time. He had to be quite old to have grown so massive, and to have earned the respect and devotion of so many full blooded demons.

Sarain watched and waited uncomfortably as this master demon stared down at her with his fiery yellow eyes. He studied her for some time; her physique, but mostly her face. She started to grow uneasy with the way he looked at her, questioning herself why she was there, as she avoided his gaze.

"Look at me," he demanded vigorously, but when Sarain didn't comply, he grabbed her by the chin with his clawed hand, and forced her head up until her eyes met his. After a moment, he let go of her, and said, "So you are the one who has been causing me trouble. You have been killing my men for a while now, haven't you?"

"They were killing mine," Sarain muttered out.

The beast looked at her and laughed to her astonishment. His laugh sounded like a deep rumble, almost a roar. Sarain didn't find what she said amusing. But then the beast stopped laughing and said, "You know you are all just cattle. You really shouldn't take offense."

"Weren't you cattle at one time?" Sarain spoke looking up at him.

"Maybe so, but I evolved from that long ago, and now even the shepherds bow down to me," he stated with conceit, then added, "And soon they will bow to you."

"What?" Sarain said with alarm.

"You have proven yourself a worthy opponent, but I would rather have you on my side, and my army still needs a general," the master demon preached, sending shockwaves to Sarain's core.

"No," she yelled and then desperately asked, "Why not Winston, doesn't he already run your club, and do your dirty work? Why not make him your general?"

"Winston is a loyal servant, and I admit, with that charm of his he can lure in anyone and pull off just about anything I ask him to. But he simply lacks the skill and passion of a great warrior, he is too busy with those cattle whores of his to really see the greater picture," the beast explained to her.

Sarain sighed as her stomach churned, "So I'm to become a vil sang?" She asked him already knowing the answer.

"Yes, but you will be so much more. A regular vil sang is just a man infected with a virus, but one of mine is someone who has been conditioned and pushed to the brink of insanity, and once that is achieved then they are turned. And this allows the demon blood to run its course more rapidly, so that the subject can reach its full capabilities," the master explained with a gleam in his already burning eyes.

"And an army of these monsters is your great dream?" Sarain spoke with a hint of sarcasm.

"Ruling over and openly of mankind is my dream, the army is just a tool for achieving that goal," he said with annoyance in his voice.

"So then you plan to drive me crazy 'til I call you master?" Sarain said with resentment.

"You will call me Sephor, with those who will also sit with me at my table," he said to her in almost a loving manner.

"You would have to drive me crazy to get me to willingly sit with you, Sephor," Sarain stated mockingly.

Sephor glared at her, displeased, and looked as though he was ready to hit her, but then stopped.

"Not able to hit a woman?" Sarain asked disdainfully.

The massive beast looked down at her. Though he was frightening, Sarain had lost the reason to be frightened. What more could he do to her that would be worse than her greatest fear of becoming a demon?

Sephor leaned down to Sarain's ear, and said in the lowest tone that his bass-y voice could go, "What would be the point of hitting you before you're about to be broken; what my servants will do to you will be far much worse."

He raised back up, and gave her one last glance before departing from the room. The other demons soon returned, and one of them carried a strange head device in his claws. They forced Sarain into the odd device and she learned that it was for keeping her eyes open and her head straight. The demons switched on the television set, and images of beasts torturing people in that very room came on the screen. Sick methods of torment were being afflicted on some people, while others were being killed and eaten; it seemed that not everyone was a candidate for transformation. Sephor wanted the weaker to be weeded out, and only the stronger to remain as his soldiers. The unwanted ones were consumed as slowly as possible and often in front of others who were good candidates. A lot of these tortures were done in groups, but Sarain hadn't seen any others when she had been brought in - she would be all alone.

Men, women, and even a few children played out on this tape; all showing horrible things to soon come to Sarain. She watched, but while she was disgusted, it hadn't been the first time she had seen something of this nature. The images on the screen could not match what she saw and smelled in person the night of her clan's raid; it having been done to her friends and family also made it far much worse.

A familiar face came on the screen; Nate. He was with a group and was made to watch a man being eaten. The look on Nate's face was one of pure torment and misery; a beast had physically held him in place just inches away from the man and forced his eyes to watch. Nate had screamed and cried until his eyes ultimately glazed over and a blank expression came over his face, and then he was silent. Now Sarain understood why, even as a vil sang, Nate had been so unresponsive to her that night.

Hours went by; hours of having to watch one sick mutilation after another; suffering face after suffering face; Blood, guts, and gore. Until finally the tape neared its end, then a glitch in the tape, and Kit popped on the screen, strapped to the same chair, forced to watch the same tape of senseless gore, forced to watch every minute of his brother's mental demise. Kit was crying, and trying to scream through a gag in his mouth. This had to have been filmed just hours earlier. Sarain wondered if she had been right nearby when it happened; too busy trying to find Sephor. Her eyes welled up as she watched Kit struggle to try and break free. She had failed him, and now Kit too was seemingly doomed to the same fate. Sarain watched intently to see what Kit's outcome would be, had he been deemed strong enough to be turned or was he weeded out, but the tape went black with him still just watching the screen.

Sarain's heart raced as she screamed in a panic, "What did you do to him?

Chapter 16

The demons approached Sarain as she thrashed in her chair; her strength was coming back. She screamed and fought in place as they watched, wondering where this new found energy had come from. One of the demons then grabbed something from a compartment behind her, and when it came back she saw a needle clutched in its clawed hand. The other demon moved to hold her still, and when it neared, Sarain broke her arm free from the metal clamp, that now dangled from her wrist like a bracelet, and shoved the beast back sending it crashing against a wall. Sarain then removed the head gear from her face, but before she had time to do anything else, the demon holding the needle rushed from her other side and jammed the drug into her non-freed arm.

She felt the needle break her skin and plunge deep beneath the surface, the drug surged through her veins, but she had yet to feel its full effect. What had they just given her? Was it demon blood? No, after a moment Sarain began to feel her head spin. It was just a sedative. She started to grow dizzy, though still felt able to fight. She tried to grab at her other clamp, but the demons quickly stopped her and held her down. The demons then injected her with another sedative. Sarain swayed and began to feel nauseous, the room seemed to get brighter, and a high pitch sound started ringing in her ears.

"Be careful that you don't give her too much, that's a powerful drug, and it still hasn't had enough time for it to completely kick in," Sephor's booming voice said, though now his tone sounded even louder to Sarain's sensitive ears, who cringed from its head-splitting effect. He must have come back to check the demons' progress.

"Look, now she's too incapacitated, that's no good for torture. Put her in a cell until she's had time to become more lucid," Sephor ordered them.

"But master, then she'll be too strong," one of the demons complained.

Sarain heard the sound of a scuffle that happened to be Sephor striking the demon, and then was followed by him shouting, "How dare you question my orders! If she is stronger then use more men! But I want her feeling every ounce of pain! Now take her to a cell!"

Sephor was about to leave when Sarain finally muttered, "What did you do to Kit?"

He stopped and said, "The boy? Oh yes, him," he turned to one of his servants and stated, "Put her in his cell." Sephor left without further interaction.

The demons unclamped Sarain, who was now limp and woozy, and took her by the shoulders. They dragged her out of the den and down the hall to a cell that lay in a particularly dark corner. They opened the loud groaning door and threw her in without consideration. Sarain fell flat on her side into a puddle, which was followed by her hearing the door slam shut and lock behind her.

The cell was dark and cold. Sarain's eyes weren't focusing or adjusting to the darkness anywhere near as fast as they normally would. She laid there wet on the ground and unable to move for a while, blind to her surroundings.

Sephor said something about Kit, was he there? Sarain was too weak to act, but managed to call out faintly, "Kit?" The room was silent, so she tried again a little louder and said, "Kit, are you there?" But there was still no answer.

She struggled to lift herself up and crashed back down on her first try. She lifted herself up again and started to slowly crawl, searching around the small cell with her hands. She bumped into a wall then used it to steady herself. She leaned against the wall and dragged herself along it, feeling for any sign of Kit. Her hand landed on a shoe, she felt up it and found it attached to a leg.

"Kit?" Sarain spoke with some alertness.

She moved forward and put her hand on his chest. Her hand laid there for a moment before she realized that he wasn't breathing. Sarain began to panic as she moved her hands up towards his face, but her hands stopped at his neck. His skin felt like ice, but more importantly, Sarain could feel the bulge of something that shouldn't have been there. A bone was protruding in his throat; his neck was broken.

Tears began to sting in Sarain's eyes. No, no it wasn't Kit, she told herself. She took his head in her arms and held him in a cradle. She looked down at his face, and while her vision was still somewhat out of focus, she was able to see enough to know that it was him. The tears ran down her cheeks, and a wave of grief and guilt fell over Sarain. Her sobs took a hold of her, and her body began to shake. A sour knot started to rise from the pit of her stomach, and Sarain turned away and vomited. Chills surged throughout her, and she clenched her teeth to keep herself from crying out. It didn't help. Sarain screamed and wailed until her throat ached.

"Bring him back!" Sarain called out to some unseen entity, "He was just a boy!"

He was a boy she had made smile; she didn't make people smile, but Kit did and he seemed happy to be in her company. Now he would never smile again, never sit with her to a meal, never come to her with a bad dream, never make her feel at home after a long night of hunting. She wanted him back so badly, she swore she would be better this time, and not just a guardian; she would be his mother. She just wanted one more chance to make things right.

Her cries went unheard and unanswered. With all she had done over the years; everyone she saved, and all the horrible things she had to see, why couldn't she have this one prayer answered, she wondered, hadn't she earned it? What was she fighting for if demons still remained with no retribution in sight for her?

She closed her eyes feeling just as damned as any other beast she fought. Everything she had ever cared about had been ripped away. No more would she fight for a higher purpose, any blade she may choose to wield she would do so to serve her own intentions.

An hour went by, Sarain laid with her back against the wall, still holding on to Kit. The drug the demons had given her had kicked in further; the room spun and even though it was dark, she could see bright colorful spots dancing around the cell. They looked like flowers, and Sarain thought that maybe they were souls; one was Kit, another was Nate, and the pretty red one was Ariana, her mother. She wasn't sure who the other ones were, perhaps members of her clan, or maybe they were people she failed to save. There were so many colors, just like a flourishing garden. Were these flowers for her?

Sarain felt very dizzy, and she was growing sleepy. Was she dreaming? Maybe she had been asleep all this time, where was she really? Sarain felt like she was forgetting something, was it time to get up and feed Kit? Kit? There was something about Kit she needed to remember. What was she holding?

Sarain let go of whatever was in her arms and it slumped to her side with a thud. She shifted to her side and fell over. I have to wake Kit, she thought to herself. Kit, no, Kit was dead. Dead.

Sarain's eyes began to tear up again; Kit was dead. It repeated in her mind over and over again, but it still didn't feel real. How could he be gone? The colors were gone, and Sarain just laid there spinning on her side. She wished the room would stop moving.

Just then the door made a clanging noise and creaked open. A voice quietly called out, "Sarain?" Was that her imagination? "Sarain," The voice said again.

"Orran?" she deliriously answered back, thinking to herself, who was that?

The door opened further, and a figure stepped in. Sarain's eyes began to focus on the man, and when she started to realize who it was they responded as if reading her mind; "Sarain, its Winston."

Winston, she thought to herself, go away. Why was he here?

He moved toward her, and Sarain hadn't the strength to move away. Winston knelt down by her, and started to pick her up, but Sarain tiredly swatted at him causing him to accidentally drop her. She fell to the ground.

"Go away," she told him, weakly.

"I'm here to help," Winston tried to reassure her.

"No, you burnt down my house. You killed Kit," Sarain said trying to be forceful, but only sounding helpless.

"I swear, I didn't have anything to do with that," he pleaded.

He tried to pick her up again, but Sarain swatted at him once more saying, "No, I don't believe you." After a second of silence, she finally said, "You're a demon; you're all planning on torturing me. You just want to know if the drug is wearing off."

"No, really, I'm here to help," he stated again.

She then started to get up on her own while muttering, "I don't want your help."

Sarain swayed and got to about half a stand when she finally collapsed and passed out. Winston knelt by her side again, and scooped her up easily this time. He lifted Sarain up, and held her in his arms. He pushed the cell door the rest of the way open with his shoulder and stepped out sideways so that he could fit Sarain through the doorway. He listened to make sure that the demons he had sent away hadn't returned; it was quiet. He carried her down the hall all the while thinking, I have to get her out of here. He hoped that he wouldn't be caught, but he knew that after this he wouldn't be able to return; surely they would realize what he had done, and then he would be hunted by them just the same as Sarain. She would be his downfall.

Chapter 17

Her eyes opened to a dark cluttered room. There were boxes stacked around her and dirt was on the floor. The air smelled musky like old books, but it still smelled cleaner than her cell. Sarain sat up with a groan. She was considerably less dizzy than she was before, but still didn't feel like her old self.

"You're awake," the familiar and surprised voice of Winston spoke then added, "I thought that you'd be out much longer."

"Where am I?" Sarain asked, looking around in confusion.

"You're in a warehouse, downtown; I didn't know where to take you that was safe," he answered her nonchalantly.

"You carried me here?" she questioned.

"Yes," he said simply, figuring that it was an obvious answer, but then realized that perhaps she was still a bit confused from the drugs. He then continued to talk by saying, "You were pretty out of it. It looks like they messed you up bad."

"You mean your people?" Sarain said while beginning to examine her injuries.

"They're not my 'people'," he responded back, bothered by her remark.

"They're demons, you're a demon, and you live and work with them; so I would say that makes them your people," she pointed out, not really caring to how Winston took her comment.

"They kill, I don't. Besides, I'm the one who got you out of there," he said in his defense.

"Yeah, right after you led them to my house," Sarain replied, getting annoyed with Winston's inability to take fault.

"I wasn't involved in the raid on your house; I was followed the night I went to talk to you. I didn't even learn of the attack until it was already too late, then I heard they had captured you and were keeping you in the dungeon. They were going to put you through Sephor's process," Winston explained.

"I know, he wanted me to lead his army," she muttered with disgust.

Winston looked a bit shocked, as though he didn't know Sephor's full plans for Sarain, and then he responded, "You must have made quite an impression on him."

Sarain was silent, Winston looked over at her expecting her to comment back, but her attention was not on him. She was looking at her shoulder, where her flesh had previously been torn off by claws; it was now caked in dry blood.

"They really tore you up good, I'm surprised that you're able to move around so well," he said observing the amount of blood that was on her back.

Sarain remained quiet for another moment before finally saying, "Don't get any ideas about my blood." She had said it gruffly without looking at him, never breaking her attention away from her wound. She was trying to pull down the clothing from her shoulder and examine the wound at the same time, but it wasn't working, her sleeve kept bouncing back up and it was apparent that she wasn't going to remove her dress in Winston's presence.

"Do you need help?" he asked moving towards her.

"Don't touch me," Sarain quickly said, her attention finally shifting to Winston. She watched him for a while to make sure he didn't come any closer to her before she looked back at her shoulder again. She started rubbing and picking at the dried blood.

Winston observed her for a minute then said, "You probably shouldn't do that, the scab needs to heal properly or else it's going to scar." He stopped talking once he noticed the dried blood flaking away and that clean untouched skin was underneath. Winston could have sworn the wound looked worse, but since he hadn't been there when she received it nor had he gotten a close look, he figured that perhaps it was just mostly smeared blood on her back. But now he couldn't even see a wound from which the blood could have originated from. He thought about the night when he had talked to Sarain outside her house, she had moved well for having a stab wound, and he was unable to see a scar on her head from when she cut it open. He contemplated it over before saying, "You don't heal like a regular human, do you?"

Sarain looked up at him, but didn't answer; she felt that he had no business knowing her family history. She tried to ignore him, but felt his eyes still on her waiting for an answer. Finally she replied, "What would you know about being human? How long has it been since you've been one?"

Winston thought for a moment then answered, "It's been a long while," he left it at that.

Sarain gave him a glance and then asked, "What were you, twenty-five, twenty-six at the time?"

"Twenty-eight, but I've already more than doubled that now," he said in response.

Sarain felt a little weird sitting there talking to a vil sang like an ordinary person, but then again, nothing about her life was ever like that of an ordinary person's so why not sit and converse with a demon. Besides,

Winston was quickly proving himself to be unlike any other vil sang she had ever met. She didn't know how to take it, but she wasn't ready to let her guard down with him. She was curious to what angle he was playing at.

"Have you worked with Sephor long?" Sarain asked him, genuinely intrigued to know.

Winston wondered if Sarain had meant the question as another insult, but didn't hear any harshness in her tone so he answered, "Just for the last few years; he needed someone to front his club."

"So why you?" she asked.

"I had been doing that kind of work since I was human, so he had learned of me by reputation; I've always found it easy to get what I want by saying and promising others what they needed to hear. Most people are easy to read like that," Winston replied honestly.

"Is that what you're doing with me? Saying and doing what you think I want?" Sarain asked him with a blank gaze.

Winston looked up at her, Sarain had no problem being upfront with not trusting his motives, this was obvious, but his answer was truthful when he told her, "I can't read you."

An awkward silence grew between them as Sarain found herself beginning to believe what he was telling her. She tried to blame it on a momentary lapse of judgment, and scolded herself in her head, telling herself that this was what he does, he had even just admitted so. Still, she was curious to know what his answer would be to, "Why did you save me?" Then she realized that she had said the question aloud.

Winston just looked at her then started to talk when suddenly the sound of boxes crashing to the ground stole their attention. Someone else was in the warehouse. They quickly rose to their feet and looked in the direction of the sound. A group of demons stood behind where the boxes had been stacked, it was unclear how long they had been there, but their attention was very clearly set on Winston.

For a moment Sarain had thought she had been once again set up by Winston, who had just been playing another game until one of the demons, a short scaly demon with big red eyes, said, "The master was hoping not to find you with the girl, but I suspected otherwise. I always knew your dirty little half blood was too human."

It was evident that Winston was no longer with them, like he had said. The group of demons was fairly large, and Sarain was without a weapon. She also wasn't sure that her body was healed enough to fight at her usual strength. She definitely couldn't take all these demons in a battle, she just hoped that Winston could fight, and with the demons approaching, she would soon find out.

Chapter 18

Two of the demons quickly rushed Winston, but the short demon, which had done the talking, held back. He appeared to be leading the others, and Sarain recognized him as the beast she had seen Sephor talking to earlier when she had eavesdropped on him in the strange arena-like room. Sarain saw him motion two beasts towards her while saying, "Grab her and bring her back to the lair." The small demon turned to the remaining group and ordered, "Stop wasting time and hurry up and kill him. Night is almost over."

The rest of the group quickly followed after the others and began flooding Winston, attacking him like rabid animals. Though Sarain was too busy to be concerned with Winston's outcome, the demons sent after her were grabbing at her arms and trying to hold her down, but they had nothing to bind her with and soon found that her slender arms were slipping from their grasps. One of the demon's claws scraped up her arms, digging into flesh, but Sarain hardly noticed the pain. She swung her leg around kicking the monster in its jaw, and causing it to lose all hold on her. The other beast took her distraction as an opportunity to rush her from behind, but she swung her arm back and knocked the creature back with incredible force. It crashed into a stack of boxes, which came tumbling down on top of it. Sarain then jumped on her other attacker and began beating the demon with her fists, pounding it into a bloody mess. Its skin was hard like a slick shell, much like that of a beetle. She let out all her pent up frustration on the beast and started screaming at it as she pulverized its face and chest till her own hands began to bleed. The creature stopped moving beneath her, and it was unclear if she had beaten it to death or just into unconsciousness.

Sarain took a shaky deep breath, with the sounds of scuffling nearby, and remembered Winston. Had he been able to take on the group of demons? Her thoughts were interrupted when something swiftly grabbed her by the arm and yanked her up. She spun around ready to fight whatever it was, but stopped when she recognized Winston. He was a little cut up, but more or less alright. Sarain found herself surprisingly relieved to see him, something she never would have thought she would be, but with times like these he was the closest thing to a friendly face. His presence there showed that she may still have a chance of escaping this alive.

Sarain noticed that some of the demons laid on the ground while others still fought in a dog pile, unaware that Winston had slipped out. These creatures really were stupid, she thought to herself.

Winston tugged on her arm, snapping Sarain back into reality, and said, "Come on, we got to get out of here right now."

She nodded and followed Winston out of the warehouse. Outside was still dark, but the sky was growing bluer; dawn was approaching. Normally Sarain wouldn't leave demons still alive if she could help it, but there were far too many for her or Winston to kill. They had no other choice but to run. The demons would soon notice their escape and be on their scent trail and with morning coming soon, Winston would no longer be able to run. Given the sun would also hinder the demons from following, but it would likely trap or take Winston completely out of commission.

Sarain knew she could always leave him behind, after all, he was just another vil sang; she herself had killed many. But she felt obligated to help Winston as he helped her; he wouldn't be running for his life if he hadn't saved hers. Though she couldn't understand why a creature, evil by nature, would betray his own kind for someone who hunted them.

Still, their fates seemed sealed; demons could follow a scent like a bloodhound. It would take an act of god to pull them out from this mess.

As they ran down deserted alleyways past crumbling buildings, Sarain knew that they could take no refuge in any place without being followed. Dawn was nearing, and she began to see the desperation in Winston's face. He didn't have much time left.

Then a rumble came from above, but not that of a demon, it was that of an incoming storm. The sky instantly broke down with heavy rain, soaking them both.

To Sarain, the water felt like it were trying to wash away the horrible experience of her capture, but to Winston, he knew that the heavy down pour would wash away their scent; with this they could escape.

Sarain turned to Winston as if reading his thoughts; now they only needed somewhere safe to hole up in. They stopped to figure out their location and Winston surveyed their surroundings.

Meanwhile, Sarain couldn't help looking at him, and wondering why he had went so far to save her; why save her at all?

After a moment, Winston seemed to recognize where they were. Then he noticed Sarain's gaze, she looked him in the eye for a moment; his eyes were a vibrant blue, but didn't glow. She had never realized how human vil sangs could be; she was so used to always seeing the demon in them. But now with her violet eyes being the only abnormal pair there, she was the one looking supernatural.

At that instant, Sarain suddenly became aware that she was staring, and quickly turned her head, then said, "Do you know where we are?"

Winston nodded silently, a little shaken, then replied, "Yes, and I know a place that we can go."

He studied her for a second, wondering what she could be thinking, and with a question in both their heads; were they still enemies?

The storm blocked out most of the sun, so when Sarain and Winston finally arrived at their destination it was nearly dawn, but the sky was still a darker shade of blue. Sarain recognized where they were, they were at the Velvet Rose.

She looked up at the building, completely drenched in rain, and turned to Winston and said, "If I was able to find you here, don't you think Sephor's men will be able to too?"

Winston looked back at her, he noticed that she had said "Sephor's men" and not his people, but he didn't want to bring attention to it, he had a feeling that it would only make Sarain revert back to her old ways. Instead he told her, "I know people know I come here, but trust me, it's a safe place."

Sarain shrugged, and thought why not hide out at a brothel, her life was going so great at this point.

They went inside, right through the front door. Sarain hadn't seen the lobby on her first visit, just a whole lot of Winston and a few other people. The lobby, to her, looked very tacky, like a cliché brothel in some cheesy movie. There was red shag carpeting, maroon and gold wallpapering, old plush-looking sofas, table lamps with colored veils over the lampshades to dim the lighting, and vases full of roses on nearly every end table. The room smelled of perfumes and freshly burnt incense.

There was a woman sitting at an old desk with a cherry wood finish. She had blond hair and looked to be in her twenties, she was attractive, but wore too much makeup, and her clothes looked too binding to Sarain; like the woman was trying too hard to be sexy. The woman smiled at Winston like she knew him, then turned her attention to Sarain and gave her a funny look.

"Now you're bringing your own girls?" the blond woman said to Winston.

"I am not his girl," Sarain quickly said, a little too defensive.

Winston chuckled at the thought, and joked to the blond woman, "I figured that I would help you recruit, being your best customer and all."

The woman laughed, but Sarain wasn't finding any part of their conversation funny. Winston chatted with the woman further; while eavesdropping, Sarain learned that the woman's name was Alorea, who had gotten up and walked over to Winston, and was now standing next to him as he explained a vague version of their situation. It was obvious the woman knew what Winston was, and she didn't appear to be scared. He told her that both he and Sarain were on the run from some very unfriendly acquaintances and that they may come there looking for them, and that they would need to be kept hidden.

Sarain began to step away, bored with their conversation, but Alorea quickly turned to Sarain and said, "Please don't track water all over the carpet and furniture."

Sarain rolled her eyes and stood in place. She would hate to ruin such a wonderfully cheap looking room, she sarcastically thought to herself.

Then Alorea continued her conversation with Winston, Sarain noticed that she would touch his arm every so often while talking to him. How much more obvious could she get?

Sarain ignored them, and looked down at her clothing, she was now very aware that she was still wearing the same revealing red dress she had worn to the club to blend in the night before, no wonder the woman had thought she was another working girl. The dress was now dirty and caked with blood. It was severely torn on the back and leg area of the dress, she must look like a mess, she thought. Sarain didn't really care how she looked; she just wanted to get into something cleaner and less showy. She was still soaked and dripping, and she assumed Winston was too.

And as if reading her mind she heard Winston say to Alorea, "Could you have someone get us some towels?"

She rang a small hand bell and another attractive young woman entered the room, this one a brunette, who asked Alorea what she needed. Alorea instructed her to get towels for Winston and his guest.

Sarain then interrupted by saying, "Could you also get me a change of clothes?"

Winston turned to her and said, "It's a shame really," referring to her damaged dress, "I think you look good in red."

Sarain hoped he was kidding, but when Winston got into his cocky attitude sometimes his comments were hard to read. She ignored his remark, and he went back to talking with the blond. After a moment the brunette came back with two fluffy white towels, and a silky green dress draped over her arm that looked like a nightgown. She handed Sarain the gown, who was thinking how the dress was not what she had had in mind. And then she wrapped the towel around Sarain, touching her shoulders in the process. Sarain flinched when the woman did this, not expecting or used to human contact, and everyone appeared to notice. The brunette looked at Sarain a little shocked by the reaction, and then looked at her directly in the eyes, which Sarain had been trying to avoid. The brunette gave her a peculiar look once she noticed her eyes, and Sarain quickly looked away. The brunette backed off and went to Winston and wrapped his towel around him as well.

Winston continued to chat with Alorea for a moment longer until finally she said, "You both must be tired. I'll show you to a room." She led them down a short flight of stairs, and into an underground level of the building that Sarain hadn't realized was there. That would make four floors total to the large brothel. She walked them down to the end of the hallway and stopped at the last door on the left.

"This is your room," Alorea said and began to leave without further instruction.

Sarain quickly looked up with a sudden thought and said to Alorea, "Wait, we have to share a room?"

Alorea stopped down the hall, turned around and said, "We are often quite busy, we can only spare the one room." She then continued to leave.

Sarain looked to Winston who was smiling at her, and she said to him, "There is no way I am sharing a bed with you."

Chapter 19

Sarain pushed open the door and began to step into the room, but then abruptly stopped. Inside the room was a dresser and attached to it was a large mirror.

She turned to Winston and said, "Do me a favor, and cover that mirror."

Winston walked inside and sat on the bed then replied, "I think I've done you enough favors lately. If you have a problem with the mirror, take care of it yourself."

Sarain groaned and muttered, "You are absolutely good for nothing." She went over to the bed and grabbed one of the extra folded up sheets on the end. She then walked over to the mirror and threw the sheet over it without looking directly at it. The sheet mostly covered it, but one end of the sheet was still wrinkled up causing it to not completely fit over the mirror. When Sarain looked up to fix the sheet she caught a glimpse of a reflection in the mirror that wasn't hers. But she wasn't alarmed; she knew that it wasn't going to be herself that she sees. She quickly fixed the sheet, covering up the helpless eyes that looked back at her.

Winston was watching her; curious to know the reason for her aversion to the mirror, but Sarain knew that he wouldn't be able to see it. That was a burden for her alone. He chimed in from the bed, "I thought us vil sangs were the ones who were stereotyped into supposedly not liking mirrors. With that whole myth of us not having reflections, I really want to know who makes that crap up."

"I'm sure you're a big fan of mirrors," Sarain replied with a hint of annoyance.

"As a matter of fact, I am. It's nice to see that I haven't aged, and to have something that will always show me the truth," Winston responded.

"Well the truth is the problem," she stated and then said lowly, "And I don't need to be constantly reminded of it."

Winston gave her a funny look before saying, "You really do have image issues, don't you? I don't see why, you could easily clean up well if you tried."

"Why should I care how others perceive me?" Sarain asked.

"So that others will love you, and respect you," he answered.

"That kind of love will get me nowhere. Besides, attachments only make things worse, or have you already forgotten what happened to my last companion?" Sarain said roughly.

Winston was quiet for a second, it was clear that he had hit a sore spot with her. But he finally broke the silence by saying, "It still isn't healthy to isolate yourself like that."

"I'm not going to take advice on what is healthy from a demon, especially one whose former alliance is out to kill him and whose only real companionship is from a bunch of whores," Sarain jabbed back.

"At least I'm living life," Winston responded, getting a little angry.

"Yeah, and taking them too," she insultingly remarked.

"Hey, I've told you before, I have willing participants that work out a lot better than killing people," he said in defense.

"You're the one who said that you enjoyed a good kill," Sarain pointed out, referring to a much earlier conversation.

"That was just to get you riled up," Winston explained, "Besides how many perfectly innocent vil sangs have you killed? Or do you stop to ask each one whether or not they kill humans?"

"Honestly, I don't care," Sarain said harshly.

"If that was true then why didn't you kill me that night when we were last here? It would have been an easy shot," Winston pressed on.

Sarain glared at him, but didn't answer. She herself didn't know why she hadn't just killed him that night. Perhaps it was because the girl he was with would have been a witness, or perhaps it was because she still had questions that needed to be answered at the time. Either way, at that moment Sarain was wishing that she had gotten rid of Winston then, because maybe then she wouldn't have gotten her life in the deep mess that it was in now. And perhaps Kit would still be alive.

Sarain noticed Winston's hands begin to shake. They may have been shaking a while, but with the argument she hadn't noticed sooner. He was trying to hide it, but Sarain abruptly asked, "Now what is wrong with you?"

Winston didn't answer right away, he waited for a moment as though judging whether or not to tell her before ultimately answering, "I haven't fed in a while."

"Well don't look at me, get it from one of your whores!" she demanded with a look of disgust.

Winston shot her a look of discontentment, then got up and stormed out of the room. Sarain felt glad to be alone, finally. She grabbed a spare blanket and pillow, and laid them down on the floor against the wall; she wouldn't risk taking the bed, she didn't want to take the chance of Winston crawling in next to her.

She changed into the silky green nightgown-like dress the brunette woman earlier had given her. It was somewhat revealing, but clean and not torn. She threw the remains of her old dress in the corner, in a pile with her damp and used towel. Sarain looked at her arm where a demon had clawed her skin just hours ago; it was already healing nicely, and would probably be gone once she woke up after a good day's rest.

Sarain laid down into the little bed she had made herself. She was exhausted, it had been a long night, and Sarain was already finding it hard to believe that just the day before she had had a home, and she had had Kit. It's funny how much could change in twenty-four hours, though Sarain found no part of her life humorous.

A wave of emotion came over her that she had been trying to hold back, but now that she was alone she let it come out. Tears ran down her face and quiet sobs escaped her lips. It had been easier to accept a life alone before Sarain had met Kit and been reminded of what it was like to have a friend and family. All these years she had never let another person get close to her since her clan's destruction. And now all her fears had suddenly been proven right; everything she cared for would always be ripped away from her.

Sarain cried herself to sleep, unaware of the eavesdropping ear on the other side of the door, listening in on her sadness.

Sarain watched helplessly from her hiding spot as her grandfather stared up at the powerful vil sang. There were demons all around, and even if he managed to strike down this seemingly unstoppable beast, the others would surely flood him. But for now the demons waited, watching to see their leader at work.

The massive vil sang stepped slowly towards her grandfather, who raised his sword in response, but the beast made no motion to raise its own blade. Instead, to Sarain's surprise, it threw its weapon down. The beast then shifted its head and gave her grandfather a peculiar look, and then even more strangely, it spoke.

"You know why we're here," the creature said in a strong voice.

But her grandfather wouldn't let the beast finish, he didn't want to hear the monster's words. He rushed the demon; lunging toward it with his blade thrust forward. He flew through the air at incredible speed, even at his age he was still a skilled warrior.

The vil sang stood frozen, like he was accepting the attack. But then with a swift blink of the eye, the beast had her grandfather's throat in his hand. He had caught the man in midair.

Sarain's heart raced with panic, the beast had moved so fast that she hadn't seen him move at all. She screamed inside her head to do something; jump out, distract the beast, try to save her grandfather; but she remained unable to move, completely petrified.

The demon raised her grandfather up to his eye level, and looked him straight in the face. Her grandfather still held his sword, but didn't use it. He stared the beast in its eyes like he was hypnotized, or perhaps just scared stiff. The demon then brought him closer, and did something Sarain found especially disturbing; he smiled at her grandfather: A smile full of razor sharp teeth. And with another quick motion, he bit into her grandfather's throat and completely tore it out with its jaws. His blood sprayed everywhere; on to the beast, into the air, on the ground, and onto Sarain's crate. His blood dripped down between the wooden panels, and landed on her arm where it ran down her skin. The urge to vomit rose up in her throat, but she swallowed it back down.

The demon threw down her grandfather's lifeless and mangled body, and the others raced to it and began feeding on the remains. They were like vultures fighting and slobbering over the meat. Sarain closed her eyes and covered her ears hoping to drown out the sounds of flesh ripping away from bone.

Sarain wasn't sure how much time had gone by before she finally looked up to see that the beasts had picked her grandfather's bones clean. Now they were searching among the other bodies, making sure there were no survivors.

A spiky scaled demon neared Orran's body, and Sarain cringed at the thought of seeing his corpse consumed. But the creature suddenly lifted its head up, moving away from the body, and began sniffing the air. It stepped toward her, following the new scent, until its eyes landed on her crate. She trembled once she realized that it knew she was there. She had no weapon in hand and no one left to save her.

Its clawed hands began to reach for the crate's lid.

"Sarain, wake up!"

Chapter 20

Sarain opened her eyes to see a frantic Winston trying to shake her awake. Panic was in his eyes, and Sarain knew that it had to be for more than just concern over her struggling in her sleep. Alorea stood waiting in the doorway, a look of impatience on her face.

Finally Winston explained, "There are vil sangs upstairs looking for us!"

"Are you sure?" Sarain groggily asked.

Alorea stepped forward and replied, "They're pretending to be regular men, but I can tell the difference. They keep sniffing the air."

Sarain looked at Winston and stated, "I thought you said we'd be safe here."

"And we will if you just hurry up!" Winston pressed anxiously.

He took her by the hand and yanked her up out of her floor bed, then rushed her out of the room. A couple of women went in to the room after them to clean and discard of any sign of them, and anything with their possible scent on it. The smells of strong perfume oils floated from the room, incense was burning, and Sarain realized that the place was kept smelling so strongly of fragrances to mask the smells of others. Whether it was a hygiene thing or not, the aromas would definitely cover over any trace of their scents. Alorea led Winston and Sarain across the hall to a small storage closet. Sarain had seen a few of the rooms before and knew that they were generally the same sizes. The closet seemed out of place. Then Alorea went to a large cabinet shelf, and pushed on its side until it rolled away. Behind it was a small hidden room. In the business of a brothel, the women were constantly finding times when they would have to hide important clients, and this was what this room was for.

Winston stepped into the small dark room, and tugged on Sarain's hand to follow. She looked down realizing that Winston still held her hand and jerked it away from him. She went into the dark hideaway, and Alorea closed up the entrance with the cabinet behind them. They waited there in the dark while the vil sangs searched the large brothel. They couldn't hear any signs of them yet, but it would only be a matter of time before they would come sniffing around the storage closet.

The room was tiny and Sarain could feel that Winston kept bumping into her. "Stand still," she whispered to him, then with a sudden realization she asked, "Can't you see perfectly fine in the dark?"

"Sorry," he quickly responded, instantly stopping.

Sarain slowed her breathing to keep quiet. Then the sound of the storage closet door opening echoed in her ears. Someone was rustling around on the other side of the cabinet, searching and sniffing for any sign of her and Winston.

After a minute another set of footsteps entered the small closet, and was followed by a voice asking, "Is there any sign of them?"

"No, they're not here. Winston must have found another place to hold up in, we should check all the warehouses," a voice replied.

"If that is what Garnok orders; he was looking into anywhere the girl might go," the first voice said.

"I hate taking orders from that little bastard," the second voice stated.

The two men then retreated from the room, but Sarain and Winston remained waiting silently. They had to wait for Alorea or one of the other girls to come back with an all clear.

The room was pitch black, but when Sarain shifted restlessly she caught a glimpse of something blue behind her. Winston's eyes were glowing, probably from the fear of getting caught. But the image of it made Sarain uncomfortable; she didn't need a reminder of her unpleasant company. She tried to ignore him, but he took notice of her reaction. Winston closed his eyes as they waited, but Sarain never looked behind her again to observe this action.

Eventually Alorea came back, moving the cabinet away to let them out. Sarain stepped out first, with Winston following soon after. They both looked to Alorea who explained, "They finally left. They searched all over, tore apart some rooms, and scared a lot of customers."

"Did they hurt anybody?" Winston asked with concern.

"No, just the business. I think some clients won't be coming back," Alorea replied with stress.

"Maybe we should leave," Sarain suggested.

"No, they shouldn't come back, and they would have searched here regardless," Winston responded.

Alorea nodded in agreement with Winston, she appeared to be quite a fan of his. Sarain wondered if Winston had ever been a client of hers, and was curious to how many of these women he had slept with. Were they all willing to satisfy the needs of a vil sang?

Alorea brought them back to their room, which had been cleaned; Sarain's self-made bed on the floor had been picked up, and the sheet covering the mirror had been removed. Sarain avoided looking into the mirror, and without being asked, Winston automatically took a sheet from the bed and covered the reflective glass. Alorea looked at him puzzled when he did so, but didn't ask why. He gave Sarain a quick glance as though seeking a sign of approval, but she looked away when they made eye contact. Something about the action, even though it was an act of kindness, didn't seem right to her, perhaps it was the fact that he was being kind.

Alorea excused herself to tend to her customers, still trying to calm the frustration from the disturbance that the vil sangs had caused, leaving Sarain alone with Winston. He went over to sit on the bed then quickly asked, "Did you want it?"

Sarain looked at him confused, and shook her head no, saying, "I don't know what has gone on, on that thing."

He laughed and sat down, then said, "They are actually very sterile here. These rooms are kept cleaner than your average hotel."

"Well, I'm not big on hotels either," Sarain muttered.

The room got quiet, and Winston waited a moment to see if Sarain would say anything else before he finally spoke again, "You really aren't a big talker, are you?"

"I don't hang around people," she said faintly.

"Why is that? Because you can be around people without getting close to them, if that is what you're worried about," Winston asked.

"I prefer not to be noticed. It's better for my line of work," she answered.

"Well you stand out more than you realize," he said being observant.

The silence was uncomfortable, but the conversation was making Sarain even more uneasy so she decided to change the subject by asking, "What are we going to do now? We can't hide here forever."

"I thought about that, you should leave town. Sephor's not going to stop looking for you, so it's better if you get far away quick," Winston instructed.

"I don't think I can do that," she told him.

Winston gave her a puzzled look and asked, "Why not?"

"I can't leave knowing what he is doing, and with what he did to Kit. I have no reason to run," Sarain explained.

"Even with knowing that he plans to turn you?" he questioned her further.

"I would kill myself before he'd have the chance. But I have to try and stop him, regardless of how large his army is," she declared.

"Well your best odds would be to destroy the club. Destroy the hive and the bees will scatter, then it will be easier to pick them off one by one," Winston advised her, "Do it during the day, when they will all be forced to go underground. I can get my hands on some explosives. The further you can get it in, the more likely you can take some of them out in the process. Now there are other exits besides the club, but those can only really be used at night, and it's at those exits that we should wait to start picking them off. But even still, it will be dangerous."

"I'm not worried about that, but why are you so willing to help me?" Sarain asked with curiosity.

"I'm just helping myself, they are after me too now, and the sooner I can get Sephor and his army off my back, the sooner I'm a free man," Winston replied.

"They weren't on your back until you helped me," she noted.

"Maybe, but I wasn't free. Sephor had me doing his dirty work, and once he got his hooks in me, I was to forever be stuck doing whatever he would ask of me. It wasn't like I was just some employee who went home at the end of the day, I was his slave," he enlightened.

Sarain hadn't seen it that way before, she had always figured that since Winston was half demon he had to be a villain, but perhaps he was just another victim. Like Nate and like Kit. This made her wonder about the rest of Sephor's army, from the tape she had been forced to watch in the tunnels, she had learned that Sephor was driving his people crazy before turning them; there was no volunteering, but now as brainwashed vil sangs, they acted on orders without further thought.

"How did Sephor start and choose who would be in his army?" Sarain asked Winston.

"Well, he started by collecting up regular vil sangs, not those robotic versions he's making in his dungeon. He promised people like me power and protection, you know, strength in numbers. Once he lured us in he started up The Purge, and used it to bring in your more unfavorable cliental. He liked criminals, because they were already prone to violence, and wouldn't be missed when they went missing. Then before I knew it he had a hoard of full blooded demons helping him turn these criminals with his 'special' method. It was like these demons popped up overnight, following his every command like he was truly one of their own. I've never seen anything like it before," Winston relayed, a little fearful.

"I have," Sarain muttered with the flash of a colossal beastly man in her mind. After a minute she asked him, "What else can you tell me?"

"Well, he uses his blood to turn each and every person. He likes to sweep in and choose his 'children', as he puts it, after each batch of torture. He likes to turn and torture them in groups, so they bond with their pain and also so they get numbed by being forced to watch," he replied.

"What about the club employees?" Sarain wondered.

"They're completely legit; all human. The club needed to appear like any other. And the employees were to be left untouched, and they were to have no knowledge of the demon activity; Sephor couldn't risk his plans getting out," Winston explained.

"What about Nate?" Sarain asked, remembering that he had worked there.

"Nate?" Winston repeated, at first not recalling name, then after a moment a look of recognition came over his face, and he said, "Oh him. Yeah he was an employee, he was still kind of new, and didn't know the club rules too well. Like if the office door was closed during club hours that he shouldn't come in, but he did one night, and saw one of the other vil sangs coming out from the hidden door under the desk in there. You know the one. Anyway, he tried to play the whole thing off like he didn't see anything…"

"I saw nothing," Sarain mumbled, recalling a dream. Winston stared at her oddly after she spoke those words, enough so that she asked him, "What?"

"It's just that he kept repeating that phrase over and over even after they dragged him down into the tunnels," he relayed still looking at her strangely.

Sarain wasn't surprised, it wasn't the first time that something she dreamt turned out to be factual, but she shrugged it off to Winston, not wanting him to know this about her, and said, "Well, it sounded like the likely response. Continue."

So he did and added, "Anyway, once Sephor found out about it, he wasn't willing to risk the kid talking. So he had him taken to the dungeon and put in with the next batch of 'crop'."

Sarain nearly found herself laughing; everything that had happened, all that had led her to this moment was because Nate opened a door. If he had just left it alone, there would have been no trail for her to follow. Who knows what Nate even thought the passageway led to; she severely doubted that he would think it was to a demon lair. If Sephor had just let him walk instead of having him brought down below, things probably would have stayed normal, and Sarain would have never troubled him.

It was funny how one simple act set off a chain reaction of events.

Chapter 21

It was two hours later, Sarain paced in the room, back and forth, waiting for Winston's return. After some more conversation, Winston had decided to hit up his connection for the explosives; they hadn't decided when exactly to go with the plan, but knew they should do it soon, and that they needed to be prepared first.

Sarain waited and worried for his return. If this was going to work then Winston would be essential to her plan, and she couldn't risk him getting caught now. He was taking longer than she expected, and with each minute that went by, Sarain was becoming more edgy of this plan with all the possible loop holes of things that could go wrong.

A knock on the door broke Sarain's train of thought. Was it Winston? No, in walked one of the women. A brunette, the same one from the night before.

She stepped into the room and softly said to Sarain, "I thought you might be hungry; you've been here for a while and haven't eaten."

Sarain searched her thoughts and realized that she hadn't eaten for more than a day. So she nodded and said, "Yes, I guess I could eat something."

And to her surprise she watched as the woman pulled back the collar of her shirt, exposing an old bite mark.

"What are you doing?" Sarain abruptly asked.

"Letting you feed," the brunette answered in confusion.

"I am not a vil sang!" Sarain shouted at her.

The woman let go of her collar and stammered, "But you're with Winston, and your eyes!"

Sarain felt completely appalled to be mistaken for a demon. She yelled at the woman saying, "I am not 'with' Winston. As for my eyes…" Then she realized that that was exactly what she looked like; with her strange feature and her unholy company, she herself would have easily mistaken her for a vil sang. So she softened her voice when she finally finished by saying, "My eyes are just my eyes. They're because of something else, and not because of 'that'."

Sarain was finding that perhaps she stood out so much when trying to blend in, because she was more than human. The people in her clan were trained to be and do so much more than what the average person aspired to. And even her own mother had achieved such a high honor when she was born with the ability to heal, something Sarain could only do to herself, unlike her mother who could heal anyone of many different afflictions. Her clan had worshipped her mother, not only for being the chief's daughter, but for delivering them from so many ailments. It was an extremely grievous day when she died.

And now there was Sarain, daughter of a healer, granddaughter of a chief and great warrior, sole survivor of her clan; it was no wonder why she didn't fit in. But still, getting mistaken for a vil sang was disturbing to her.

Sarain looked at the woman, who stood there awkwardly, and grasped that there was something else about this brunette, other than her ability to make Sarain uncomfortable, that had been bothering her in the back of her mind. And after seeing the old bite marks on her neck, Sarain realized what is was, this was the woman she had seen Winston with that one night.

Sarain wondered if the woman had feelings for Winston. She hadn't greeted Winston or shown him any special interest the night before in the lobby. But in the moment she had stated that she thought Sarain was with him, Sarain had noticed a look in the woman's eyes, like envy.

The woman never appeared to recognize Sarain, so she must have never seen her that night, and Sarain's staring was making her uneasy, so Sarain finally asked her, "Could you bring me some real food?"

The brunette nodded yes to her and quickly left to do so. Sarain sat down on the bed and took a deep breath. There was so much that needed to be done, and she hated having to hide there and wait. She knew that it was probably only a matter of days until she took on Sephor's army, and even with Winston's help, she couldn't see the fight being successful. There were too many; more than two people could take. She knew that even a clan of warriors couldn't take on a properly trained demon army. But this wouldn't stop her from trying. She would fight till the day she died, even if the day was soon.

Sarain wondered if Winston would stay fighting by her side or if he would run; perhaps he had already fled. She was still waiting for his return, and he had been the one to bring up running. Winston might not be coming back.

Another hour went by, still no Winston. Sarain had eaten, but the food had been delivered to her by another woman, a red head; the brunette must have been too embarrassed to come back. Sarain found it a bit amusing that a woman in such a line of work would get embarrassed so easily.

Sarain had asked for yet another change of clothes. This time she was more specific for comfortable non-revealing clothing. But the red head told her that they didn't have anything like that lying around, the best she could do for her was a robe to cover up with. Sarain put it on and was at least glad to have something on over the thin silk of the nightgown she wore.

Sarain looked up at a clock on the wall, it was half past ten. She couldn't sit around anymore, she had to do something. She got up, and went for the door. Her hand reached for the knob, when it suddenly turned, and the door opened. Sarain jumped back to miss the swing of the door, and standing on the other side was Winston.

"Oh" he said a little surprised, "Were you leaving?"

"I got tired of waiting," Sarain replied, then added, "And I wasn't sure that you were coming back."

He looked slightly disappointed, but said, "I wouldn't just abandon you like that. I know you need my help, even if you are too proud to admit it." He walked into the room, closing the door behind him, and said, "I'm sorry it took so long, but dynamite has to be transported carefully. Besides, I also stopped to get you this."

He held up a bag, and then tossed it to Sarain. She caught it and looked inside. It was a plain black shirt and black slacks. Winston smiled at her and said, "I figured that was more your taste than that enticing number you've been wearing."

Sarain gripped her robe shut; she knew that nightgown would bring unwanted attention, but she was grateful for the modest clothes. She looked up at Winston and said, "You didn't have to do that."

He shrugged and replied, "Well I needed you to be in something that you could fight in. I also picked us up some weapons."

"Were you followed?" Sarain blurted out immediately.

"I don't think so, besides, they probably think that we've left town. It would be the more logical thing to do," Winston said like he was trying to persuade her.

"Well then they don't realize just how dedicated to my mission I am," Sarain stated while staring down at her new clothes.

He gave Sarain a worried look that she didn't see, and replied, "I guess not."

Chapter 22

Sarain dressed then let Winston back into the room. The clothes were a size too big, but they worked a lot better than the overly feminine stuff the Velvet Rose had to offer. She felt like she could breathe better now, no longer so self-conscious.

"I'm ready if you are, to do some hunting," Sarain spoke with an energized tone.

"Maybe it would be better to wait until tomorrow, so that you can set up the explosives during the day, and then we'd have a whole night of time to fight the survivors. I just think that we shouldn't take the risk of having anyone see us and find out that we're still in town before then," Winston suggested hoping to calm an eager Sarain.

She thought it over for a second, then sat down next to him with a huff, and said, "You're probably right. That does make more sense. It's just hard to sit around doing nothing, especially at night."

"I know what you mean," Winston stated.

"Well then what should we do?" Sarain asked, and then quickly added, "That isn't what you normally do here."

He smiled and joked, "Well that would certainly pass the time, but if that isn't an option than maybe we should just talk. If I'm going to be fighting by your side, I might as well know more about you."

"There isn't much to know," she abruptly replied.

Winston gave her a discouraged look and said, "I seriously doubt that. Why do you have to be so guarded?"

"I just don't want to talk about myself," Sarain answered while getting up. She paced the room a bit, and then sat down on the floor against the wall across from Winston, on the other side of the room.

It was obvious to him that she was trying to distance herself, and he seemed bothered by it, but he didn't press on. He just moved the conversation along by asking, "Is there anything about me that you'd like to know?"

Sarain contemplated that question, and answered, "How did you become a vil sang? I mean, why?"

"Well, I was twenty-eight, and the idea of growing old was looming in my head. Friends of mine we getting married and starting families, and all I could think was that I didn't want the party to end. I didn't know about demons or vil sangs, or anything like that. I just met this attractive woman one day, who told me that she could make it so that life didn't have to end. She said she could give me something. I thought she was talking drugs but…"

"She gave you her blood, right?" Sarain said finishing his sentence for him, it was the obvious answer.

"Yes," he said while nodding, and continued, "After that I felt sick for a while; the demon blood was taking over, and it wasn't until then that she explained what was happening. But I didn't fully understand. I knew that I was getting stronger, but I didn't realize that I would have new weaknesses. She told me to avoid sunlight, but I didn't know about holy relics. I wound up burning myself on an old crucifix that I used to like to wear; I couldn't even pick it up anymore. I got mad at her for not telling me beforehand what was going to happen, and I guess I complained too much, because one day I woke up and she was gone," Winston paused, reflecting over his past, and finished by saying, "I never heard from her again after that."

It was a harsh thing to do, Sarain thought, but also in the back of her mind she thought of how immature Winston must have been to do something like that. She kept that opinion to herself.

Winston gazed at her, wondering what she was thinking, and decided to ask, "Are you ready to tell me something about yourself yet?"

Sarain glanced over at him with a frown on her face, but didn't answer. So instead Winston simply said to her, "Something stole your innocence, didn't it?"

She looked up at him from her position on the floor, and thought about not answering, but she heard the words escaping her lips anyway, "No... I don't think I was ever innocent."

He lowered his eyes and commented, "It must have been pretty bad."

"...Yes," Sarain plainly muttered. She left it at that, and gave Winston a look not press on further.

They were quiet. Sarain hoped not to be questioned any further; something inside of her just wouldn't let her share her past with anyone. Dreams and visions of her past were one thing, but there was something different and almost unbearable about putting the story in her own words. Like once it escaped her lips then she would truly have to live with it; keeping quiet made it feel less real, like a bad nightmare.

Winston watched as Sarain looked lost in thought. He had answered her questions, but she still avoided his. No matter what he did this girl seemed untouchable, even when she openly hated him he still couldn't get under her skin; befriending her hadn't made much difference. Nothing was able to penetrate through the brick wall she had built around herself. He wondered if she had been any different with Kit; had she loved the child? Or was he now just another brick on her wall? Winston didn't know if he admired her for her strength or pitied her for her isolation from life. But he did know that she was the perfect example to show that great strength only truly came with great loss. She was carrying a wound that wouldn't heal. Winston wished that there was something he could do to help her, and wondered if his presence had any effect on her.

Sarain glanced over at Winston, sensing his stare. Why does he keep watching me, she thought to herself. Time was inching by feeling never-ending. Should she just try to sleep, get her rest? His eyes are still on me. She looked over at Winston; he was blatantly staring at her with his eyes so blue. Why does he keep doing that? Why has he done any of the things that he's done towards me? Helping her, rescuing her, visiting her at her house, even kissing her at the club, at the time it had seemed like he was mocking her, but now she wondered if it had been something else completely. She wasn't sure if she was ready to hear the answer, but she had to know, so she found herself asking him, "Why have you never tried to kill me?"

He looked a little surprised by the sudden question, but answered, "I don't like to kill."

"But wasn't it your job to protect the club?" Sarain asked.

"Yes, but…" Winston started to say, but didn't get to finish. Sarain interrupted him by quickly pressing on with, "Well, then why didn't you just kill me? I know you had the chance."

"I…" he began to say while searching his thoughts, and finished with, "I don't know why."

Sarain gave him a confused look, thinking, what kind of answer was that? She tightened her hand into a fist at her side, beginning to get annoyed with Winston's averting; at least she was straight forward about not wanting to answer questions, besides how could she trust him if she didn't know his motives. She would get truth out of him, one way or another.

But before Sarain could continue to drill Winston, something else snatched her attention; a woman's scream coming from upstairs. She quickly exchanged glances with Winston, who then pulled out the weapons he had purchased earlier, two katana swords.

He handed her one while saying, "I figured this would be a step up from that machete you used to carry."

Sarain took the blade, and then a deep breath; it felt good to have a weapon in her hand again, but she still worried as to what they might find upstairs.

Chapter 23

They raced down the hall and up the stairs toward the continuous screaming. There in the lobby, Sarain first noticed the brunette woman, whom she had talked to only hours earlier, lying dead on the floor. Her throat had been torn out and now she lay sprawled out in a puddle of blood; for a woman who was willing to feed vil sangs, she had learned the hard way that not all vil sangs were willing to show restraint.

Standing nearby Sarain saw a vil sang trying to bite at Alorea, who was the one screaming. She was frantically thrashing and swatting at the vil sang trying to break his grip off of her. Sarain rushed towards them raising her sword and sliced the demon down its back. Alorea then successfully shoved him away, and Sarain gave one final blow towards his neck, decapitating the man.

Winston also ran to help one of the girls who had two vil sangs attacking her. The girl, a red head, was on the floor trying to kick them away. She had gone to the brunette's aid earlier, but couldn't help her and was the vil sangs' next target after the brunette fell. Winston pulled one of the vil sangs off of her and threw him back, then ran another one through with his sword who was in the process of biting her. The girl screamed and rolled away from the impaled creature. She gripped her neck which was bleeding, but was otherwise alright. The second vil sang lunged at Winston while he was trying to pull his sword out of the other. It threw its weight at him, knocking him to the ground, but the force was enough to get Winston's sword out of the other vil sang's back, and he still held the blade tightly in his hand. Both men scrambled up, but Winston moved a few paces quicker, and was up before the other vil sang. He brought back his katana and sliced it through the air at the attacker, cutting his head clean off.

Winston turned toward Sarain and Alorea then called out, "Are you alright?"

Alorea stammered trying to catch her breath, then managed to get out, "Upstairs...More of them...Chased after the girls and clients."

Winston hurriedly ran towards the higher levels of the building, and Sarain looked at Alorea and the red head and said, "You two need to go downstairs and barricade yourselves in one of the rooms. They haven't gotten downstairs yet."

The girls nodded at her and quickly went running for the stairs. Sarain took one last glimpse at the brunette on the ground, definitely dead. She wondered if this bothered Winston, he had been intimate with this girl, and now she was gone. But it was still unclear to Sarain whether or not he had had any real romantic feelings toward the woman. By his lack of a reaction towards the sight of her corpse, Sarain would guess that he had no real ties to the woman, and she didn't know if that was because of the vil sang in him or the man.

Sarain darted down the hallway. She didn't know which floor Winston was on, but she figured she would start on the first floor she came to. The first couple of rooms were empty, the two after that had dead vil sangs whom had already been dealt with. The next room had a dead half-naked man on the floor, apparently a client who was unable to fight off his attackers. Sarain could hear whimpering coming from a closet in that same room, and she opened the closet door causing the young blond woman inside to yelp.

"It's okay," Sarain immediately said, "Go downstairs to the basement, some of the other girls are waiting down there.

The girl looked a little relieved and ran out of the room. Sarain continued to search through the rest of the rooms on this floor, but found the rest of them clean; Winston had already come and gone through here. She ran up to the next floor, but then continued on up to the third floor, the last one. She figured that either Winston was taking care of the second floor or would have already done so, so to be of use, she decided that it would be best for her to move on ahead. Besides, Winston seemed perfectly capable of taking care of himself.

Right away, once Sarain reached the top of the stairs, she could hear a man and a woman screaming. She rushed toward the sound of the screams and ran into a room where a couple was being attacked by three vil sangs. The man was screaming for the vil sangs to take the girl and leave him alone, but the demons weren't interested in that deal. They attacked him too, and one of the vil sangs was already biting at his neck. Another had a knife to the girl and was cutting at her leg while lapping up her blood. The girl continued to scream as the third vil sang sank his teeth into her neck. Sarain pulled the vil sang that was biting the girl's neck back by the head just enough to get her sword into position to cut off his head. Soon after, the girl stopped screaming and appeared to have passed out from either shock or the loss of blood.

The man, noticing Sarain's attempt to help the woman, called out to her from beneath his attacker and cried, "Help me!"

Sarain grabbed the vil sang on him and threw it back against a wall with ease. The human man gave her a frightened look, surprised by her strength, and then took off running from the room. Sarain then turned to see the third vil sang hurrying toward her with the knife. She dodged it, but was grabbed from behind by the vil sang she had thrown off the man, whom had already scampered back up. It tried to bite her but she leaned forward and swung her elbow back and up against its jaw. One of its fangs scraped her arm, but the vil sang still stumbled back losing its hold on her. The demon holding the knife came at her again, and she heaved her sword at him. It pierced through its throat, but it kept on moving at her. She needed to fully decapitate him. She grabbed at the knife with her free hand. It grazed her palm, causing her to bleed, but she got a hold of the blade and yanked it away from the vil sang. Then with a quick tug, she finished chopping off his head. The remaining vil sang grabbed at her waist from behind again, and tightly wrapped his arms around her, giving her little room to maneuver. She squirmed to break free, and started to be able to turn around, when the vil sang suddenly dropped to the ground.

Sarain spun around to see Winston standing behind her, having just killed the vil sang attacking her. She was relieved to see him, but made no effort to tell him so, instead she went to check on the girl she had saved earlier. The girl was covered in blood down her neck and all over her arms and legs; she was unconscious, but still had a pulse and was lightly breathing.

Sarain turned and looked at Winston, and asked, "Is the rest of the building clear?" He answered, "Yes." And Sarain then said, "We need to move this girl then."

Winston stepped forward, leaned in, and took the girl in his arms. He followed Sarain, who carried both swords now, out and down the stairs. They went to the basement floor to find the other girls, and after Winston called out to Alorea, they opened up one of the bedroom doors. A few more girls had found their way down to them, and with the one Winston carried, that left six still alive. Apparently ten girls worked there, which meant there were a few more dead upstairs that Sarain was unaware of.

Alorea looked glad to see Winston as she tended to the unconscious co-worker. She gazed at him with such affection in her eyes, seeing no connection between him and the other vil sangs who had just attacked the Velvet Rose. Sarain watched as Alorea stared lovingly at Winston, who was too preoccupied to notice the attention. Instead, Winston approached Sarain, looking at her hand, and asked, "Did you get hurt?"

Sarain looked past him at Alorea, who seemed saddened to see Winston standing with her, while she responded, "It's just a scratch, I'm fine."

"Good," he said to her with a smile.

One of the girls then chimed in by asking, "Why did those men attack us?"

Sarain looked up at Winston and muttered, "Was it because of you?"

He shook his head, and said, "I don't think so, they weren't even looking for me just now."

"Then why?" Sarain asked, knowing that vil sangs were cruel, but usually didn't attack on groups of people.

"I'm not sure why," he answered with a sigh.

Suddenly in the distance, they started hearing more screams. The women didn't seem to notice; only Sarain's and Winston's sensitive ears could pick up on it.

They told the women to stay there, waiting in the room, as they went back up to the lobby to investigate.

When they reached the lobby, everything inside still looked as it did earlier; furniture was knocked over, the brunette still lay dead on the ground. But they realized that the screams were coming from outside.

They approached the outer door, and could see a car crashed into the building across the street. The driver of the car lay on the ground by his open door, bleeding from the neck. People were running out of buildings, screaming, and a few bodies were in the street. Then Sarain noticed that some of the people who were running around had glowing eyes.

She quickly turned to Winston, and said with a revelation, "Sephor set his army loose!"

Chapter 24

Sarain and Winston rushed out into the cold night air, both with a sword in hand, and started running to people's aid. Sarain first reached an elderly woman wearing pajamas and slippers, and was cowering on the ground as a vil sang prepared to bite her. The vil sang held on to the woman with one hand, and that was the first thing Sarain rectified. With one swift move she chopped off the creature's hand. The elderly woman fled in terror, while Sarain continued to hack at the once man, who had been so taken by surprise with her attack that he did little to defend himself.

Winston went to save a man who the vil sangs were trying to drag out of his store. He was a big man, but against two vil sangs he didn't stand a chance. The shop owner screamed as the men dragged him through the broken glass from his store window. Winston charged at them and swung away. He killed one vil sang right away by chopping off his head, the other let go of the shopkeeper and lunged at Winston. The vil sang knocked him back and he stumbled, but didn't fall. He plunged his sword into the beast's chest, stopping it instantly.

Sarain hurried to the aid of a couple; a man was trying to fight a vil sang off his girlfriend who already had one bite mark on her shoulder from the attacker. Sarain pulled the woman away from the beast and shoved her towards her boyfriend. Sarain yelled for them to leave after she noticed the boyfriend still trying to help, and they ran towards a car Sarain assumed was theirs. She swung her sword at the vil sang who jumped back to miss it. The vil sang's eyes glowed, but when Sarain looked into his face she saw no life in it. He seemed robotic and much like Nate had been when she fought him. He had to be the result of Sephor's special vil sang process, acting on an order to kill rather than just the regular demonic urges. She also noticed that his reflexes weren't as good as a normal vil sang; it was as if the lack of free will gave it less meaning and strength to fuel it. Sarain quickly took down the beast and others more after it.

A little more than two hours had passed by with Sarain and Winston constantly fighting off vil sangs, until finally their numbers dwindled. Sarain walked down the street alone heading back towards the Velvet Rose; she had been up and down streets and in stores finding and killing vil sangs. She saved some people and also found quite a few casualties as well; throats had been torn out and people had been fed on. Sarain did what she could, and ended up killing nearly forty vil sangs herself so far. It was a busy night, more than any other night she had fought before, but these vil sangs did fight sloppy, unlike the ones she normally faced. They didn't fight with a strong will for survival, and often left themselves open to attack.

While Sarain had been clearing out a house, she had come upon two children hiding in the corner of a room. Their parents had been killed by vil sangs before she had arrived, but she managed to save both boys. The younger one, about five, reminded her of a younger version of Kit. She knew it wasn't him, but for some reason saving the child felt like she was doing some sort of justice for Kit. The children had stammered out a thank you to Sarain, but she knew that they would have a hard life as orphans ahead of them, which left her feeling disappointed that she had not arrived a few minutes earlier to save the parents.

Sarain glanced around the dark street as she walked, holding her sword tightly. It was quiet, the screams had stopped a while ago, there was no one left around to scream; some people probably still hid, but many had fled and others lay still unable to ever scream again. Sarain scanned her surroundings for Winston, they had gone their separate ways while fighting, but now that things had calmed she looked for him amongst the wreckage of the battlefield. The vil sangs had only appeared to have attacked the slummy downtown section of the city, it was isolated and no police came to the rescue. Sarain figured that the whole attack would probably be written off as some kind of gang war.

She then realized that she was only slightly worn after the battle, and this began to make her think of how the fight had been too easy. Had Sephor really bred that weak of an army?

The sound of a door creaking open caused Sarain to look over at a small apartment building. The door was opening slowly, and Sarain began to raise her blade, but stopped when she saw blond hair and the familiar face of Winston step out from behind the door. He had been clearing out the buildings in the area, and had finally finished with that particular building. His eyes quickly located and settled on Sarain, and he looked relieved to see her. He had a few scrapes on his arms, but otherwise looked alright; he also found the battle a little too easy.

Sarain approached Winston, with her sword down and his lowered as well. He gave her a smile as she neared and stated, "I guess you really can hold your own," he stared down into her eyes adding, "I'm glad to see you've made it through this okay."

Sarain looked up at him and asked, "Is that it? Because it feels like something is missing."

Winston gazed down at her for a moment, before fully realizing that she was talking about the vil sangs, after which he instantly cleared his focus and answered, "No, there were no demons, just vil sangs... That had to only be the first wave of attack."

Sarain nodded in agreement and said, "Then we should probably go ahead with our plan tonight before Sephor lets any more of his army loose."

"It'll be more dangerous this way," Winston spoke trying to make her fully aware of her actions.

"I don't care," Sarain replied, "We have to stop him before he hurts more people."

Winston nodded and walked back with her to the Velvet Rose where the rest of their supplies still waited.

Sarain wasn't scared about what lay ahead, but Winston felt a ball of fear forming in the pit of his stomach. He glanced at Sarain through the corner of his eye and worried that he wouldn't be able to protect her.

Sarain stared up at The Purge, it looked so small and quiet now; no one would imagine the vast amount of horrors that lay underneath it. Sarain held a container of gasoline, and both had their sword strapped to their backs. Winston carried the explosives; he looked at her as she stared at the club.

"You have the keys, I'm just waiting for you to open the doors," Winston said to her. He had given Sarain his keys to the place earlier. Now she held them in her hand as she approached the doors. She put the key into the lock and turned it. It opened; the demons must not have thought to change the locks, they probably didn't think Winston would be so bold as to come back.

Inside the club was dark, they hadn't been open that night; Sephor probably didn't see much point in it since he had bigger plans. No one waited for them inside, and Sarain wondered if Sephor had them gathered down below, going over plans for another assault.

The room was big and empty, and to Winston it seemed strange; he had once worked that room, spending hours at that place, and now he was about to destroy it. Sarain saw the room and was reminded of her failures; getting captured, getting wounded, losing Kit. It was outside the front doors that Sarain had first met Winston, the beginning of a chain of events that would later unfold; she never would have guessed that he would later help her destroy the place. She had pegged him all wrong, she didn't think a vil sang could change its ways and become good. And she was actually glad to have been wrong this time.

They headed for the office, but stopped short when they heard the rustling sounds of someone behind them in the door way. They both spun around and saw the large man who always guards the door, standing in the entrance.

He saw Winston and said, "I've been waiting around for someone to open the club. No one came to the door today." He then noticed the supplies that they carried, and an astonished look came over his face, "What are you guys doing?"

"Go home, Ron," Winston said to him in a stern tone.

Ron, the guard, gave him another look, then quickly glanced into the club, and finally turned and went down the stairs of the club outside. He didn't ask any more questions or come back after that, his respect for

Winston made him not question what he did.

Winston and Sarain went resumed heading to the office. Sarain had to unlock the door to it, and inside the room was dark and deserted. The demons weren't guarding the club at all; they must have used one of the other exits when the wave of vil sangs was let loose. Sarain worried that more demons would get out from those exits once the fires started, but she and Winston were only two people, and this was the exit that they chose to cover. As long as they managed to take out the mass, the escapees would be easier to pick off.

Sarain went over to the desk that she remembered being heavy and lifted it with ease. She felt as though she had gotten stronger since the last time she had come this way. Winston went into the tunnels first; they had agreed, since he knew the layout better he would lead the way, and also since he was carrying explosives Sarain would go down with him and fight off any potential problems they may run into while he set up the explosives. They would have to get the explosives down deep into the tunnels, near the center of the catacombs, which happened to be near Sephor's chambers. The destruction, the blaze, and the all-out collapsing of the tunnels should be enough to stop most of the demons, but it was likely that some would escape, and those were the ones that Sarain and Winston were prepared to fight.

Going down the spiral staircase felt especially long this night. Winston kept setting up a few bits of explosives long the way. Sarain half expected for them to slip up and make a loud echoing noise or have someone jump out at them at any moment. But no one jumped out, and not one mistake was made. Sarain thought about the last time she remembered being on those steps, she had been racing up them hoping to save Kit, how long ago that seemed now. They reached the end of the stairs, and were now close to their target, but "now" was when everything would get riskier; the demons had to be nearby, and would hear any loud noise they may make. And there would be a chance they could be stumbled upon by accident.

Winston made a right at the base of the stairs toward the hallway that led to Sephor's chambers and to the dungeon were Sarain had been kept. She wondered if Kit's body still waited in the cell. It didn't matter, there was no life left in his body, and a burial would be meaningless to her. It wouldn't change anything; it wouldn't change the fact that he was gone.

Sarain followed Winston in the hallway till he stopped where the hallway split off. He turned and nodded downward to her, letting her know that this was where he wanted to put the rest of the explosives. He set them down and started connecting pieces together. Sarain didn't know what exactly he was doing and didn't know how he knew how to work explosives, and she didn't ask; it didn't matter to her as long as they got the job done.

She stepped past Winston as he worked, and tip-toed over to the door that led to Sephor's auditorium. Then she realized that she could hear voices coming from the other side. The demons must be in there at this very moment, which must have been the reason why they hadn't run into any during their infiltration.

Sarain put her hand on the door's handle then looked over at Winston, he was watching her, and when they made eye contact he nodded "no" to her. He knew what she wanted to do. Sarain looked back at the door, and continued with her urge. She opened the door, just slightly and silently. She peered through the newly made crack, and could see a mass of demons, mostly full blooded, sitting around with their attention all settled on something down below them. She could hear the booming voice of Sephor talking, but couldn't make out all the words. What she did manage to hear was Sephor saying, "Kill anyone you come across, I don't want any survivors. Don't waste time feeding, and if you come across the girl I want you to bring her to me."

Did he still want her alive? Sarain couldn't understand why, Sephor already had his army, why did he still want her? Was it just to fulfill some sort of sense of dominance over her, so that he would feel like he had won? Perhaps he didn't like loose ends, but why not just kill her then? Maybe he wanted to kill her himself. Sarain gently closed the door, she had heard enough.

She looked over at Winston who was still setting up the explosives, she hoped he was almost finished, she didn't know how much longer it would be before Sephor would set this next wave of demons loose, but she had the feeling it was soon. Finally Winston attached the last chord, and began to stand up when the door behind him, towards the staircase, opened. A vil sang stood on the other side, it was unclear if he was one they had missed earlier during the attack, just now returning, or one whom was made to patrol the tunnels. But when his eyes landed on Winston and Sarain he shouted out, "Intruders!"

Winston quickly ripped off the sword strapped to his back and sliced the vil sang down, silencing him, but it was too late, his call had rang out and Sarain could hear the shuffling sounds of demons moving behind the door she stood near.

"Run," she heard Winston shout. His voice triggered her to quickly open her can of gasoline as she ran after him; she hadn't come this far not to finish her part of the plan. As she chased after Winston she left a trail of gasoline behind her. She could hear the demons busting through the door and following after them. She forced her legs to move faster than they had ever moved before. She couldn't afford to slip up, or else it would cost her, her life.

Chapter 25

They ran up the spiral staircase, an all too familiar experience for Sarain. At least now she wasn't alone, Winston led the way. They leaped up steps, jumping over explosives they had set up earlier, and leaving the trail of gasoline behind them. Sarain hoped that the explosives would still work properly after the demons had trampled through them, though either way the gasoline should help do the trick.

They reached the top of the steps, and Winston shoved open the door leading to the short hallway under the office. He checked to make sure Sarain was still behind him then ran down the hall and threw open the door to the passageway. He used so much force that with the weight of the desk, it broke the door off of its hinges, and it and the desk went flying and crashing into one of the walls of the room above. He then waited for Sarain while fidgeting through his pocket and made sure she was up the steps before pulling out a lighter, lighting it, and throwing it down on the trail of gasoline.

He ran after Sarain who was heading for the exit. As they reached it the first of the explosions went off, one of the ones set on the stairs. They leaped off the steps in front of the entrance and went crashing onto the pavement. The explosion caused the ground to shake and a big crack to form on the building. Another explosion went off and the building began to further crumble. Winston scrambled to cover Sarain; worried that debris from the building may soon come falling. Sarain covered her ears in time for the third explosion. The ground began to groan and Winston hastily jumped up and picked Sarain up with him. He yanked her along forcing her to run with him into the street. Another explosion went off, and then the club began to cave into the ground. The roof collapsed, and the walls finally busted down. The club was caving into the catacombs underneath.

After a moment another explosion, this one larger than any of the previous, went off, and the ground shook violently. Sarain nearly lost her balance until Winston grabbed her and clung her to him. He held on to her, shielding her from the debris that came flying at them when the club finally exploded into flames.

Things began to become quiet and Sarain looked up at the club. It had been reduced to rubble, and ash covered the ground and some still came falling from the sky. The heat from the flames warmed the night air, and danced before them. To Sarain, the destruction was a glorious sight, a wave of relief came over her, and she felt that Kit and his brother could now be at peace. Winston watched as the building burned, and to him it was as though a chapter in his life had ended, it was a tale he was ready to leave behind.

The sounds of rustling coming from inside the inferno caused Sarain to move away from Winston. He watched as she moved towards the wreckage un-strapping the sword attached to her back. He didn't know what had triggered her to start checking the rubble, all he could hear was the sound of burning, but he followed after her and picked up his sword from the ground along the way.

Her eyes scanned the flames, and she could sense something coming. She thought she saw something flicker, other than the flames, and move from somewhere inside. They were coming. Sarain knew the fight wasn't over yet, and sure enough a demon emerged from the flames, then another, and another. They began flooding out from the blaze, angry and focusing their rage on the two figures standing in the street: Sarain and Winston.

A demon called out to Winston yelling, "You filthy traitor!"

The insult didn't faze him; Winston held his ground as a pack of demons flocked to him. He started slicing them off, fighting them back, as they continued to come at him. Another group of demons rushed at Sarain, charging with a furious look in their glowing eyes that she knew that there would be no more saving her for Sephor, if he was even still alive. She chopped at the limbs that grabbed at her; arms and claws flying about. Sarain swayed and shifted almost as if dancing as she swung her sword. She sliced head after head, dropping demons one after another. She was moving at incredible speed, so much that even Winston couldn't keep up with her kill count. He was fighting the demons off of himself, but was still getting scraped up with the occasional swat of a claw here and there.

But the demons couldn't seem to touch Sarain. As she spun around swinging her blade, she caught a glimpse of Winston fighting. He was still standing, and Sarain was glad to see it, but his eyes had begun to glow. Though now she couldn't tell if they were glowing from an inner demon rage or if they were just reflecting the light from the flames, something her own eyes were probably doing right now. He reminded her of her clan, the whole setting did; the fire, the wreckage, the numerous beasts. He looked like a warrior fighting to protect his people, with the same courage and the same strong look upon his face. To her, he no longer looked like a vil sang; he was a man, fighting for a better life.

A sudden wave of pain shot through Sarain's back, and she staggered forward. She could see a look of fear come over Winston's face from where he was standing, and she realized that he was reacting to her. She didn't know what had just happened, but she could feel warm blood oozing down her back. Her eyesight began to blur, as she still swung her sword at demons. Winston made his way to her, killing creatures along the way. Their numbers had lessened dramatically, but there were still a few left to fight. However Sarain started to feel herself beginning to fall back, she was heading for the ground when a pair of strong arms caught her.

Sarain thought of her grandfather, his face flashed in her mind, but it was her mother's voice she heard telling her that it was not her time yet. A bright light formed before Sarain's eyes and she could feel a gentle hand place itself on her chest. A surge of energy rapidly pulsated through her, and the bright light faded away. She now saw Winston's face hovering above hers, he had caught her. He laid Sarain down on the ground, on her side, and continued fighting the monsters around them.

Sarain flinched and finally realized that something was sticking out her back; it was a shard of debris that some demon had jammed into her back, barely missing her heart and her spine. She groaned as she reached for the shard with her hand. Her fingers landed on it and she gripped the shard. Then with a deep painful breath she yanked it out, and a blast of pain rushed through her torso. Sarain screamed out, but didn't buckle in agony, she couldn't afford to waste any more time lying there. She lurched up, and lifted her sword. Sarain noticed one of the demons staring at her in disbelief, a small scaly demon with large red eyes. She had seen this beast before, once with Sephor, and then again leading the attack when the demons had found her with Winston in the warehouse. He was Sephor's next in line. Had he been the one to stab Sarain?

Winston noticed that Sarain was back on her feet, and then followed her gaze to see what she was staring at. Garnok, he realized, that little bastard had survived the blast. It was an unfortunate occurrence that he would soon rectify. Winston made his way to the demon, chopping himself a clear path. Sarain was back to fighting, so Winston no longer needed to worry about the other few remaining demons. His sights were set on

Garnok. Garnok trembled in fear; the beast that once gave out orders so impulsively in Sephor's stead was now weak with no underlings around to direct. Winston had always hated the tiny suck-up.

Winston approached Garnok, who glared up at him; the little beast opened up his mouth and said, "I always knew that Sephor shouldn't have put his trust in you. You had too much of a weak human streak in you. You will fall just as any human, and be damned out of both realms!"

Winston had heard enough, he raised his sword and brought it down on the annoying demon. He sliced Garnok clean in half; both pieces slumped to the ground with a twitch, but with no more aggravation to Winston.

He and Sarain finished killing off the remaining demons. More may have escaped from different exits throughout the city, but they would have to wait for a different night. It was nearly dawn, and Winston had to seek shelter from the coming sun. He and Sarain both staggered back to the Velvet Rose. Both needed a long and well deserved day's rest. They were surprised to have made it out alive from the battle, and with a new day nearing, it looked as though the nightmare was ending.

Chapter 26

Back at the Velvet Rose, everyone was still cleaning up after the raid on the building earlier. The bodies had been cleared out, furniture had been picked up, and blood stains had been cleaned as best they could, scrubbed away. Sarain and Winston were winding down from their battle, tending to their wounds.

Sarain lifted the back of her shirt and felt for the wound she had received. It still felt moist; it burned to the touch and throbbed throughout. She strained to clean it; it was in just that position on the back that's hard to reach. She soaked a piece of cloth in a bowl of water, rung it out, and then put the damp cloth on her injury. It stung, and she winced. She twisted her wrist up to reach the wound, her fingers pushing the cloth upward.

Winston watched as she struggled until finally he walked over and said, "Let me help."

His hand went to her back; his fingers grazed hers as he took the cloth in his hand. She let go, and let him put pressure on her back. With his other hand, he held on to her arm to steady her. He then eased up on the pressure and wiped away the dried blood around the wound.

"This doesn't look that bad. It looked a lot worse when you got it... It scared me... But you'll be just fine with the way you heal. It'll be good in no time," Winston said reassuringly.

Sarain had listened intently, and with confusion she questioned, "It scared you?"

"Yes, I thought I was going to lose you," Winston responded with little thought as he cleaned off her back.

Sarain hesitated for a moment then lowered her shirt back down, and twisted around toward Winston, who still held onto her arm.

"I wasn't finished," he said softly, puzzled by her actions.

She didn't respond. She just stood there and looked up into his eyes, as if searching for an answer, then asked, "Why are you doing all this?"

"What? Helping you with your wound?" he unsurely replied.

"No... Yes, all of it. Why are you helping me at all?" she proceeded to question.

Winston let go of her arm and took a step back. "What's wrong with helping you?" he asked, nearly demanding.

"Nothing except for I don't know why you're doing any of it! Why do you keep helping me?" she argued, insisting on getting an answer.

"Like I told you before, I don't know why," he said looking away, trying to avoid her stare.

Sarain moved toward him while saying, "That's not good enough... Give me a real reason."

"I don't have one, I just don't know," he pleaded, raising his voice.

"Yes, you do," she shouted back, "Just tell me!"

Then in an instance of frustration, and without a second thought, Winston yelled out, "Because you make me feel human!"

Sarain was silent; she didn't know how to answer. So Winston continued by saying, "And since the moment I first saw you, all I've wanted to do is touch you." He met her gaze and said, "I tried to fight it, I tried to just do my job, but the more I was around you, the more I couldn't help myself." He stepped toward her, and then added, "I have to be near you. I have to have you in my life."

Sarain put her hand up to stop Winston, and gently said, "Don't."

He flinched, and looked as though he were about to burst into tears. He gazed at her, hurt, his eyes questioning her, but all Sarain could bring herself to say was, "I can't."

A tear escaped his eye as he turned away. Winston nodded his head lightly and said, "Okay." He put down the dampened cloth, suddenly aware that he had kept it in his balled up hand. He went for the door, but stopped when Sarain said, "Wait."

Winston glanced back over his shoulder at her. Sarain stood there shaking and unsteady, she looked scared. She felt completely lost, but spoke anyways, saying, "Don't go." He turned around to face her, but didn't move any more than that. She continued to speak softly, "I... I've never done this. I've never been in this position. And it's just that, I can't do this with a vil sang, or anyone. I don't think I have it in me to be that vulnerable."

"You're shaking," he spoke observing her, "It looks to me like you're already 'that' vulnerable."

Sarain took a deep breath, and replied, "You might be right." She stared at him for a moment without a word, and then she started to cry. She was tired of hiding her emotions, tired of bottling everything up. Winston rushed to her and took her in his arms. She cried against him and he comforted her as he soothingly said, "It's alright. I'm not going anywhere."

Sarain held on to him, it had been so long since someone had comforted her that she was afraid that if she let go it would go away. Then she found herself reaching up to Winston and caressing his face. He was handsome, a fact the she had often overlooked. He leaned down to kiss her and she didn't stop him. His lips were soft and cool, and this time his kiss didn't leave her feeling tainted; instead, surprisingly, she felt warm. Sarain wrapped her arms around him, and realized that she wanted to feel him. She wanted to feel him everywhere. And he wanted to touch her.

Sarain opened her eyes, it was nearing night again, and she had just awoken from a long sleep. Winston lay next to her, his arm around her; he, however, remained peacefully asleep. Sarain still felt sore from the night before, but her wounds had already healed a great deal. This was her time to rest, and she understood that the worst was behind her, but the feeling of incompleteness still lagged inside her. Her mission would probably never feel finished, and this she would have to accept, but something still felt off. Like there was something she had missed.

Sarain slowly rose out of bed. Winston's cool arm dragged across the skin of her bare stomach, and she was careful not to wake him. She found the robe she had worn before and wrapped it around herself, then looked around the room to find something to help her pass the time. She debated leaving the room to see if Alorea or any of the other girls needed help cleaning up the place; it was still a bit in disarray and wouldn't be having clients for a while. Sarain hated having nothing to do.

She gazed over at Winston who was sleeping soundly; he hadn't noticed her absence from the bed yet. Then her eyes scanned the room again and she spotted something that she hadn't observed the first time. The sheet covering the mirror had fallen. It must have fallen while she slept. She debated leaving it for Winston to fix, but then thought with everything she had been through lately, what more could it really show her. So she walked over to the mirror, and right away took a hold of the sheet. She tried not to look but something still caught her eye; in the reflection a scene played out, a scene she was very familiar with.

A violet-eyed girl cowered in a box, clinching to the ankh she wore around her neck, and watching a mess of violence unfold before her eyes. She had lost everyone. Her face was full of panic and fear as a scaly demon approached her hiding spot, and with its claws it reached for the lid of her crate. Her heart raced knowing that she was now all alone with no weapon and a fresh memory of what these demons did to people. Its nails scrapped against the wood of the box, and the panels groaned as the lid was pulled away.

Sarain could feel a gust of cold air come rushing in from the new opening, and with it she knew that she had been found. She looked up at the scaly demon; he was much larger than her and his skin reminded her of a pine cone. He looked hard and strong like wood and his eyes glowed red as they stared down at her.

Without thinking Sarain stood up, there was very little point in crouching, and if she were about to die she wanted to face her destroyer. She could see that other demons were now watching, waiting for the one that stood near her to make its move. It was all an entertaining game to them, watching the kill, admiring the corpses, they didn't even seem to care that some of their own had fallen.

The beast tilted its head and appeared to smile at her, perhaps it was just showing its fangs, but it had a look about its face like it had found a prize. The demon put off a sense of smugness, and Sarain could feel herself growing angry. It was like it wanted her to be scared, it wanted to push her to the point of insanity, and only then would it be ready to kill her. She wondered how many of her people had this particular creature killed. Had it been one of the ones that fed on her grandfather?

The beast stood too close for her to have time to grab a weapon. It exhaled and she could smell the sticky sour stench of decay on its breath. She looked into its eyes and could feel herself growing hot. Its eyes glowed so fiery that she thought they would burn her, and she felt on fire. The invisible blaze around her grew intensely, and before she could realize it, she was screaming. The expression on the demon's face changed, first to one of surprise, and then to one of agony. Everything but she and the demon appeared to be spinning, and it wasn't until things began to focus once more that Sarain saw her own arm sticking out of the demon.

Her hand had completely disappeared into its chest, and now she was clutching onto its heart. How had this happened? She had let her rage take over her, and somehow found the strength to break through the demon's hard exterior with her own bare hand. She gripped her hand down tightly then ripped her arm back out. The beast's heart pulsated in her hand, and she could feel it squishing in between her fingers. The demon dropped dead to the ground while the others stood simply watching in amazement.

She could sense all eyes on her. She waited for the other demons to attack in an all-out flood fashion, but instead she heard the sound of a loud and deep horn blaring. She had heard this horn before, earlier during the raid right before another wave of attack. But this time instead of more monsters arriving, the demons began to retreat. Why were they leaving now?

The demons walked off, some even passing near, but none bothered her. She watched as they left her and the bodies behind. The demons no longer seemed to care or notice her presence. Until she felt a pair of eyes still watching her. She looked up and saw Orran's and her grandfather's killer, the massive demonic vil sang that had swept in and finished off her clan. He was staring at her; he had been watching her the whole time.

It was an amazement that this beast had ever been human with his gargoyle-like features and his fierce yellow eyes. He had not lost interest in her like the other beasts. He took a good long look at Sarain, like he was etching her into his memory, until finally even he began to walk away. They all were leaving her there, alone.

Sarain took a deep breath; it had been a long time since she had last finished that memory. But this time she saw something new; her clan's killer was not just some extraordinary beast, he had a familiar face. It was Sephor. Why hadn't she recognized him sooner? It was like her mind wasn't ready to let her see it until now. It was all so obvious to her suddenly, why the whole battle the previous night reminded her so much of her clan's raid. It wasn't just from similarities; it was because Sephor led both attacks.

Then another revelation came to her, she knew what the source of her incompleteness was, and knew exactly where she could go to find it.

Chapter 27

Sarain woke Winston and told him that there was somewhere she needed to go. He chose to come along, but didn't understand how or why she knew to go to this place. They were on the road for a short while, driving in silence with Sarain still not ready to share how she knew where to go. They brought weapons, and all Sarain managed to tell Winston was that there would be a battle.

He worried about her fighting so soon again, her wounds had not yet completely healed. He also noticed that when he would try to touch her that she started moving away again. He hoped that this was only temporary - a side effect of her focusing on her mission.

After a while of driving on the interstate, Sarain finally pulled over to the shoulder of the road. She got out of the car and Winston followed. He looked around confused; they were out in the middle of nowhere. Nothing was around for miles. Sarain grabbed her sword from the car, without a word, and then began walking into the field she had parked next to. Winston did as she did, and trailed behind her.

He wondered what could be going through her mind, while her face gave no expression to hint at what she was feeling. What had he gotten himself into?

They hiked through marsh and overgrown brush. They trekked for nearly an hour before Sarain finally stopped in the center of an open field. She looked up at the sky, it was a beautiful cool starry night, and so much different from how she remembered the place from the last time she was there. The field was empty now; no huts, no livestock, no bodies to be seen around. It looked peaceful, like nothing horrible had ever happened there. But when Sarain took a deep breath, she could feel the earth screaming. The memory was still there, like a scar that would never heal.

A rumbling noise grew with the wind, and Winston started to look around with uncertainty. He didn't know why they were there, but even he could sense that something was coming. Sarain stared on into the field, waiting for the arrival, undisturbed. Before them a mass of blue flame emerged, the blaze exploded into a dance, and it flickered both high and wide. Winston jumped back, surprised, but Sarain did not budge.

Soon the flames lessened and figures could be seen standing in the fire. Winston stared in amazement, he had never seen such magic done before, but Sarain had. Out of the fire the beings stepped out. All were large, but one specially was massive. Sarain and Winston both recognized his intense yellow eyes: Sephor. He was accompanied by three of his strongest, best demons. Winston recognized them too, he hadn't seen them too often, but knew that Sephor only called upon them when he needed a particularly demanding task taken care of. This was not going to be a simple match, and Winston doubted his ability to hold up against even just one of these beasts.

Sarain glared up at Sephor, who held back his men from attacking her. He looked down upon her like she was just a child and said, "I knew you would remember eventually, that we met before."

"Is that why you were so persistent on getting me out of the way?" Sarain asked him.

"Well at first you were just a nuisance," Sephor said in his booming voice, "I didn't suspect who you really were until I took this off the boy." He held up Sarain's ankh, she had given it to Kit, and never thought to look for it on his body once he was dead. The ankh didn't appear to bother Sephor; he was too powerful to be fazed by the trinket, something that only worked on lesser demons.

He gazed down at her and continued to explain, "I remembered seeing it on a very powerful girl one night many years ago. And since I knew the intruder was a woman, I had to see if it was really you."

"And that's why you wanted me alive so badly," Sarain concurred, understanding his plan.

"Yes, you would be the perfect piece to my collection. The only one strong enough to lead my army," Sephor told her.

"Your army is gone now," Sarain stated with a sense of conceit.

"You took them like I took your clan," Sephor remarked, pointing out the irony.

Winston listened as they conversed; now getting a better sense of why Sarain was the way she was. He felt bad for ever having pushed her limits; he had no idea what she had been through, or what she had come from. It explained how she had grown to be so strong, how she knew to do things that other humans could not. He held even more respect for her now, knowing what she had survived.

Sephor continued on addressing Sarain by saying, "I knew you were powerful, but what I didn't expect were your charms…working on my men." He looked over at Winston, who stared back at him. "He was one of my best. Really, you should have seen him at his work. He could get humans to do and give up anything, especially the women," Sephor turned to Winston and asked him, "Was she worth it? Leaving your seat of power. Does she taste as sweet as she looks?"

Sarain cringed at the thought of Sephor seeing her that way, but wasn't surprised with him being a complete monster all around. She was growing tired of his chattering; there was only one thing she wanted to know. She stepped up to Sephor, looking him in his yellow eyes, and asked, "Was all this just so that you could dominate over people?"

"Of course, I wanted more power; I was tired of having to hide in the shadows. I wanted people to openly fear me," Sephor said in his deep uncaring voice, then remarked, "But that's not what you really wanted to ask."

He was right, Sarain had held back what she truly wanted to know, and with a deep breath, she finally brought herself to say it, "Why did you attack my clan; what was it that you were trying to tell my grandfather?"

Sephor nodded, and then smiled and said, "Yes, that's it. And that's what has been fueling you all these years, hasn't it? But I don't have an answer for you."

Sarain became outraged, thinking, all this chatter and he holds back now. "Why not?!" she demanded.

"Because I didn't lead that attack, I was just a knight following his king's order," Sephor simply replied.

Sarain's heart began to break; she thought she was so close to the end only to learn that there was still someone else responsible for her clan's destruction. Sephor may have been the one to physically kill her grandfather, Orran, and others, but someone else brought him there. And she so badly needed to know who and why.

She felt her body growing hot, and with an exchange of looks they both knew there would be no more talking. The other beasts lunged toward Winston, leaving Sephor alone to take on Sarain. Winston raised his sword knowing that this would be his true test to see if he was worthy to fight by Sarain's side. She looked up at Sephor's burning eyes, and let her inner blaze help wield her blade. She swung her sword at him, using more force than she had ever used before. It came down with incredible speed and might, but suddenly stopped short.

She hadn't stopped herself, something unforeseen had stopped her. Sephor had grabbed her arm, holding the sword. He had moved at a speed that wasn't even visible, much like he did the night of her clan's massacre. Sarain's body felt engulfed in flames. He was faster than her, and she couldn't keep up. He smiled down at her, knowing that she would lose. That smugness that look Sarain hated was in his eyes. He didn't even see her as a threat.

The fire took over, and once again, Sarain was screaming. With her free arm she let go of her blade, knowing that Sephor had made the mistake of only grabbing one of her arms. She thrust her fist forward at his chest. His gray skin was like stone, but she broke through. Her fingers rushed through his insides, searching through the surprisingly cold muck. She felt it, his heart, like a rock, and grasped down onto it. Sephor roared in agony, he hadn't seen it coming; he had thought his hide was too strong for her to penetrate, but he had mistaken her for the girl she had once been. Maybe then she hadn't been ready to take him on, but now she fought on a new level, one that had surpassed Sephor.

The other beasts stopped to see their master destroyed, an error that gave Winston time to chop off the first one's head. By the time the second one turned back around, Winston's sword was already rushing toward it.

Sarain stared up at the fallen beast, his grip on her arm had already released, and the fire was fading from his eyes. He slumped down as she pulled back her arm. Sephor's eyes glazed over as he watched Sarain holding his heart. It was black, and didn't look human. He had always wondered whether it too had changed like his face. He couldn't even remember what his face had looked like before. Or what color his eyes had been. Had they been blue?

Sephor's head hit the ground, as well as the third beast's who had been charging Winston. He was dead, and Sarain stood there staring down at him. She tossed his heart aside; there was nothing left there for her to do. She picked up her ankh that now lay next to Sephor's body, and pocketed it. She was glad to have it back.

Winston approached her, slowly, and asked, "Is it over?"

She still looked down at Sephor, thinking, no, it wasn't, but instead she answered, "For now."

He put his arm around her and they walked back to the car, with Sarain all the while thinking that she never wanted to come back to this place again.

Chapter 28

On the way back to the Velvet Rose Sarain finally shared the details of her clan's destruction with Winston. He was amazed with the tale of her survival, and also found it odd that they left her alive.

"A costly mistake," Winston called it, stating how Sephor had underestimated her, and how they must have assumed that Sarain wasn't worth the trouble; after all, she was only one child.

Sarain did not shed a tear during the recount, it no longer tormented her in the way that it once had. She was quiet again after that, and they finished their drive in peace.

Once they reached the Velvet Rose, they were greeted by Alorea, who already had the place looking in order. Winston went to put away the weapons, giving Sarain one last look before leaving the two women alone.

Alorea watched as Winston walked away leaving the room, and then turned to Sarain and said, "You're a lucky woman. I wished he looked at me that way."

Sarain gave her a weak smile, it was an expression she wasn't used to using. She excused herself from Alorea's presence, and proceeded to go down to her room, where she waited for Winston to return.

Sarain stood alone in the room, and put her hand in her pocket. She pulled out her ankh necklace and examined it. She thought of Kit, and pictured him wearing it. He had been so happy when she gave it to him, but it didn't do him much good. It didn't stop Sephor from killing him. She thought about her clan, and realized it didn't help her that night either. Nor her mother who wore it before her and still wound up dying young. But regardless of its lack of effectiveness, it was still a part of her, so she put it back on her neck, and that was where it would remain.

The door opened, and Sarain turned to see Winston walking in. He smiled at her and in a cheerful tone said, "It looks like now we can truly rest."

Sarain nodded at him and smiled. His eyes lit up and he remarked, "That's what I like to see. You have such a beautiful smile."

He walked over to Sarain and took her in his arms then leaned in for a kiss, when he unexpectedly yelped and jumped back. A scorch mark of an ankh was on his chest, and Sarain realized that her necklace had burned him. He looked down at his chest for a moment and then back at her before realizing what had happened.

He shook his head then responded, "It's okay, it's just a scratch. You'll just have to take that off around me."

But Sarain did not comply; she just stood there looking at him bewildered.

Winston stared back at her for a second, puzzled, then commented, "I'm alright. Are you?"

Sarain felt like her eyes were just opening, she had almost forgotten what Winston really was. Then she thought about what Sephor had said, about Winston being one of his best. And brought herself to ask him, "How many people have you killed?"

A look of worry came over Winston face, and he answered, "I told you that I don't like to kill people."

"But that doesn't mean that you haven't," Sarain observed.

Winston shook his head at her and said, "I don't want to do this."

He started to walk away, but Sarain grabbed his arm and said, "Even if you haven't killed lately, you still lured in people for Sephor to kill. And worse, he made monsters of them!"

"Is that how you see me? A monster?" Winston shouted at her.

But Sarain ignored his question, there was one of her own that was now bothering her, and she had to ask him, "What did you say to Nate the night we met?"

Winston's eyes went wide, and he didn't answer. Sarain gripped his arm tighter and pressed on by saying, "Why was he heading to his and Kit's apartment? What did you tell him to do?"

Tears were welling in Winston's eyes as he looked at Sarain, he didn't want to respond. She shoved him back, away from her and yelled, "Tell me!"

The tears ran down Winston's cheeks and he cried out, "Fine, I'll tell you! That night, I told Nate to go to Kit and retrieve him. To bring him back to the club so that we could turn him!"

A look of disgust came over Sarain's face and Winston quickly explained, "But you don't understand, I had to tell him that! We didn't know how much his brother knew, we couldn't risk word getting out, and we couldn't have any bodies left behind!"

Sarain's hand went to her mouth; she thought she was going to be sick. Winston moved toward her, but she abruptly moved back, and shouted, "Stay back!"

He was trembling, and looked like a scared child, "Sarain," he whimpered, "I love you." Then he looked over at her with fear in his eyes and asked, "Don't you love me?"

Sarain didn't answer; she just stared at him, a cold and hateful stare. It was answer enough for Winston; he turned around and left the room slamming the door behind him. Sarain didn't know where he was going or if he was coming back, but figured that he wouldn't be back soon.

She sat down on the bed and tried to catch her breath. She wondered if she could forgive Winston for his transgressions. They were before her, and he was trying to make amends. He had fought by her side; he destroyed former colleagues, and had saved her life more than once. It should have been enough for her to forgive him, but all she could think of was the number of vil sangs they had fought together, people he was directly responsible for bringing in. There had been so many, and he had been a key figure in Sephor's army.

Sarain placed her hands on her forehead, hoping to block out the thoughts, but it didn't help. She shook her head furiously and got up. She couldn't stay there, and she wasn't going to wait for Winston to return. She had to get out, she was now feeling smothered inside, and needed fresh air. She left the room, went down the hall, up the stairs, and into the lobby.

There Alorea was sitting at her desk. She looked up at Sarain as she entered the room and asked with concern, "Is everything okay?"

Sarain did not reply she just headed for the door. She heard Alorea call out from behind her, "Are you coming back?"

Sarain walked out and let the door close behind her. She knew she would not be coming back. There was nothing left there for her. In fact, there was nothing there in town left for her to do. She had already stopped the great evil, and now she needed to move on. She didn't know which town she would go to next, somewhere far perhaps, and new. It didn't matter. She just wanted to get on with her mission, and she would be doing it the only way she knew how, alone.

Maybe this time she would find peace, and possibly an answer to why her people had to die; if Sephor couldn't tell her, then that meant that there was still someone out there who could. And she would find them. Even if it was the last thing she did...

End of Book 1

Continue Sarain's adventure in Vile Blood 2: Reflections
Available in eBook and print!

Thanks for reading!

Jen Golembiewski